# Red Tides

by the same author:

FICTION

*Our Lady of the Pickpockets*


POETRY

*Beauty is a Dangerous Thing*

*Madame Doubtfire's Dilemma*

# Dilys Rose
# Red Tides

SECKER & WARBURG
LONDON

First published in Great Britain in 1993
by Martin Secker & Warburg Limited
Michelin House, 81 Fulham Road, London SW3 6RB

Copyright © Dilys Rose 1993

The author has asserted her moral rights

'Lazy Sunday' (Marriott/Lane) © 1968 EMI United Partnership Ltd, London
WC2H 0EA. Lyrics reproduced by permission of CPP/Belwin Europe, Surrey.

A CIP catalogue record for this book
is available from the British Library

0 436 42581 5

Phototypeset in 12/15 Perpetua
by Deltatype Ltd, Ellesmere Port

Printed in Great Britain by
St Edmundsbury Press Limited, Bury St Edmunds, Suffolk

for Sophie and Cleo

# Contents

# Acknowledgements

Stories from this collection have appeared in:

*New Writing Scotland 10, Panurge, Radical Scotland, Scotland on Sunday, Scottish Short Stories 1993, Slip Roads & Off Ramps, Telling Stories, West Coast Magazine, Woven by Women*

'A Little Bit of Trust' won the Macallan/*Scotland on Sunday* Short Story Prize and was broadcast on Radio 3; 'The Mama Chorus', 'Gynae' and 'Jumping Into Bed With Luis Fortuna' were broadcast on Radio 4.

# This is Tomorrow

Though she lay with one pillow under and one pillow over her head, she could not block out the nasal warble of the disc jockey to which Frankie, who lived on the floor above, was crossing imaginary lochs on his rowing machine, his trim moustache glistening with sweat. She glanced at the luminous digits of the clock which stood on the bedside table, ticking its own small contribution to the pre-dawn chorus. It was six a.m., as she knew it would be.

It was too much, being woken again on top of the baby roaring for feeds all through the night. She pressed the top pillow hard against her ear and pulled down the blanket but now that she had been woken there was little chance of getting back to sleep again, little chance of being able to muffle the rousing words of the DJ and the brash music he fed to his early-morning listeners. To the mother, this assault on the ears was worse than any alarm clock. It didn't simply shock her awake then leave her to gather her senses but insisted, like a stubborn child, until she felt her body stiffen with a hopeless and distressing rage.

Rage was an emotion she had not really known in herself until she became a mother. Coolness had been her characteristic

1

response. Temperature control. Emotions on Hold. But nowadays rage took to bubbling out of her, like a hot thick soup, spurting its burning broth and scalding at random.

She wriggled on to her back, taking care not to disturb the baby who lay like a starfish between her and her husband, snoring softly, hogging the best part of the bed. The mother huddled on the edge. It was still dark outside when the upstairs radio was turned off. By this time she had heard – between exhortations to leap out of bed and jog round the nearest available open space – that roadworks on the M1 were causing lengthy tailbacks, that a leading brand of breakfast cereal had been taken off the market due to the discovery of carcinogenic additives, that bags under the eyes could be reduced by wiggling the nose, that commuter stress could be alleviated by early baroque flute music, that the number of hedgehogs killed on the motorways was at an all-time high, that an artificial Christmas tree was more environmentally sound than a real one. And a dozen golden oldies, songs which had been hits when she was an idle teenager: 'Wild Thing', 'Dedicated Follower of Fashion', 'Lazy Sunday':

> Lazy Sunday afternoon,
> got no time to worry,
> close my eyes and drift away,
> close my eyes and drift away,
> close my eyes . . .

7 a.m. Still an hour in which to catch some more sleep, an hour before the morning routine need be set in motion. If she could lose consciousness quickly she might feel rested by eight. But if it took too long the cat-nap would only make her feel worse when she did have to get up, so was it worth trying? She closed her eyes

and began to breathe slowly, deeply, the way she had been taught at the ante-natal refresher classes, amidst a roomful of women propped up on cushions, rehearsing for pain. But this only emphasised the tight knots of tension which snagged across her back from her neck to the base of her spine. She shifted, shifted again, rotated her shoulders, made her mouth hang open to prevent her teeth grinding together. She tried to make her mind go blank, empty.

That was what the mother was seeking, an emptiness, a void into which nothing would flow, fill up and demand attention. A clean, dry basin, with no dirty dishes in sight. But it wasn't easy to empty the mind. Not easy at all. The more she tried to clear it, the more cluttered it became, each thought jostling for attention, the essential and the junk, the things she must remember and those she'd be better to forget.

Just as she began to sense her aches and pains retreating, the tensions loosening off, the mind sifting its jumble, she heard the familiar sound of her three-year-old racing down the hall, pushing open the creaking bedroom door and skidding to a halt at the bedside. And then the high clear voice

– I want breakfast. Is this a nursery day? Is the baby in your bed, again?

– Shush. Shush.

– I'm hungry. Is it morning time? Is this a nursery day? Mummy? Mummy!

– Shhhh. You'll wake the baby.

– Is this a nursery day, Mummy? Is this tomorrow?

– No, it's today. The day you're on is always today.

And then she remembered what day it was, leaned over to switch off the alarm before it began to bleep – it would wake the baby but not her husband – and with more enthusiasm than usual, dragged herself out of bed.

Her eyes were still half-closed as she stepped into the shower. Today she must fight her craving for sleep. Today was a day to be alert, to savour each moment. She had things to do, other than washing, cleaning, shopping, cooking, feeding, clearing up. She had people to see. A life of her own for a day and a night.

– Corn Flakes, Weetabix or Honey Smacks? the mother asked, as her daughter trotted behind her into the kitchen.

– I want porridge.

– Please.

– Porridge *please*.

– I don't think there is any.

– Yes there is. It's in the cupboard.

– I don't think so.

– Yes it is. So there! I want porridge I want PORRIDGE! It was going to be porridge or a tantrum and porridge took less time so she put on a pan of milk to heat and began clearing away the clutter from the night before. As the milk frothed over the lip of the pan, she could hear the baby begin to cry, its whimpers building up to a full-throttled scream. She lifted the milk pan off the heat, stirred in the oats, turned down the gas, filled a beaker of juice for her daughter and gave her a book to look at while the porridge cooked, while she got the baby up, washed and dried its hot pink bottom, changed the nappy and dressed her in fresh clothes, threw the nightsuit into the laundry basket, slid the jiggling body into the highchair, while she filled a kettle and switched it on, found the baby's plate and beaker, cut a slice of bread for herself and put it under the grill to toast. She dropped a dollop of porridge in the Peter Rabbit bowl, added milk, sugar, spoon, set it down in front of her daughter who screwed up her face and began to whine:

– But I wanted to put in the sugar BY MYSELF!

# This is Tomorrow

– Next time, okay? Tomorrow.

– But this is tomorrow. THIS IS TOMORROW!

– This is *today*. How many times have I told you, the day you're on is always today.

– It is not! Don't you dare say that! said the child. The bottom lip was pushed out and a couple of large tears pooled in the corners of her angry eyes. The baby laughed and banged the table with a chubby fist.

– It's not funny, said her big sister.

– She's just trying to cheer you up, said the mother.

– She is not! But anyway anyway anyway how can I cheer up when I've just been upset!

As the baby girned in response to her sister's sudden gush of tears, the toast began to smoke under the grill but the mother turned it over anyway, poured boiling water into the baby's mush and – to avoid lumps and choking fits – stirred as patiently as she could. She fetched a couple of rattles from the toybox and put them in front of the wee one to keep her occupied while the food cooled. She made coffee, took the toast out from under the grill, spread it with butter and bit off a large chunk. Her daughter was dragging her spoon through the porridge, turning what had been a fairly appetising plateful into a lumpy, sloshing mess. She had not yet begun to eat. The baby was hitting itself in the face with a rattle. The mush was still too hot for the baby so the mother finished her toast, gulped down a mouthful of coffee, walked briskly through to the bedroom and shook, gently, the exposed shoulder of her husband. She shook the shoulder again, firmly. She spoke his name gently. She spoke his name firmly. She announced the time then went back to the kitchen.

Five minutes later, after managing to aim a few mouthfuls of food into the baby's roaming mouth, she returned to the bedroom and went through the shaking-waking process again. This time she was shrill. Her husband's eyes and mouth opened suddenly, as if she had dunted his skull with a mallet. His body jerked into a sitting position, then slumped back against the pillow.

　　– What day is it?

　　– My day, said the mother. My day *away*.

　　– Right, said the husband. Right. He shook himself and rolled out of bed.


Back in the kitchen the mother said:

　　– You haven't touched your porridge.

　　– My spoon has, said her daughter. You've got a dress on.

　　– Eat up now.

　　– You've got a dress on. Why have you got a dress on?

　　– Yes, I've got a dress on.

　　– Are you going to a party? Can I come too? Can I wear my party dress and my tights with the Silver Minnie Mouses on the legs?

　　– It's nursery today. I'm not going to a party. I'm going to a conference. Cold porridge tastes horrible, you know.

　　– You know, this porridge tastes horrible and it's not even cold. HA HA HA HA. What's a confrence?

　　– Eat up now.

　　– What's a confrence?

　　– A kind of meeting. Lots of people meet and talk. I have to stand up and talk. About children. You don't want me to tell them that my little girl doesn't eat her porridge? Slowly her daughter raised a loaded spoon to her mouth and turned suspicious eyes on her mother.

　　– Are the people strangers?

　　– Most of them will be.

# This is Tomorrow

– I'm not allowed to talk to strangers. Why are you going to talk to strangers?

– I'll tell you tomorrow, said the mother.

– But this is tomorrow! You said last night you were going away tomorrow!

In spite of a last-minute panic search for her purse – her daughter had hidden it inside one of the baby's socks – in spite of having flown into a rage, threatening to take off her dress, her make-up, to throw her conference notes in the bin and the uneaten porridge at the wall, with apologies and goodbye kisses and an additional load of guilt, the mother finally gets out of the house.

The train is delayed and by the time she arrives in the city it is rush hour. The portion of her day set aside for a light meal and rest before the evening event has been lost through the hold-up. The streets are dark and crowded with nudging, irritable queues of people, all trying to get home before those ahead of them. She is hungry. The small cafés have closed and there is no time for a sit-down meal so she buys a sandwich from a takeaway, cheese and ham – a striped slab of orange, pink and white and tasting of soap – and gulps it down on the way to her hotel.

The room which has been booked for her is quiet, spacious and plush, a huge bed, carpeting into which her toes disappear, chintz curtains. She has a view of the river where brightly lit ferries paddle through dark, gleaming water. The room is also very warm. The mother phones the organisers to let them know that she has finally arrived. When she has unpacked her bag, she takes off her clothes and sprawls on the bed. This is just where she wants to be, on a bed in a quiet room, with the river rolling by outside the window.

Alone. Not that it wouldn't have been good to be with Jack, her husband, the kids' father, dad. They spent so little time together, just the two of them. But it is perfect without him. At that moment he would be bathing the children, bent over the tub, shirt sleeves rolled up, steam crinkling his hair. The kids would be pink and glowing, the older one washing her doll's hair, the baby splashing and squealing with delight. Bathtime was an oasis between teatime squabbles and bedtime tears.

The mother has only a few spare minutes before she must get ready to go out and she is just beginning to enjoy being where she is. She rotates the dimmer switch until the room is lit only by a faint orange glow from the river lights. She looks up at the dark ceiling and begins to drift into an expanding, enveloping emptiness. The street noise fades into a gentle, rhythmical clatter. The radiators hum. She stretches out a hand, disconnects the phone for a few minutes of certain peace. Her eyes close.

She wakes from a vivid seam of dreams and feels refreshed. It is dark outside but she can hear birds. She checks her watch. She reconnects the phone and calls the service desk.

    – That's correct, madam.

    – Are you sure?

    – Quite sure, madam. 6.15 a.m.

    – You mean it's morning?

    – Friday morning, madam. Breakfast begins at seven.

    – But it can't be. It can't be!

She goes to the window and drags the curtain open. Across the river, against the skyline, is the unmistakable pink smear of dawn. She has slept right through the evening, the night, the whole bloody conference, right through her first opportunity to escape the laundry, the vacuum cleaner, the lifting and laying, the first chance to break through the walls of domesticity which thicken as they stand, the first occasion to take part in something bigger than the house, to invade her mind with something other than the next meal, the next stack of dirty dishes, how to negotiate a buggy and a ratty pre-schooler across cracked pavements to the grocer's, the fruit shop, post office, bank, newsagent, how to juggle the chores of the day to fit in with the variable but despotic routines of baby. She has missed the first opportunity to be a person in her own right, to have some kind of independent presence, to be more than just a buggy-pushing, bag-laden donkey.

Even if the conference had been a washout, how the hell does she explain coming all the way here – at the committee's expense – only to fall asleep? Even if her paper had been a disaster, at least she'd have done it, done something, something else, even if the party after had amounted to nothing more than chatting with other parents about the kids they'd left at home. Even going to the other end of the country she hasn't really left her own behind. They're still there, dawdling invisibly at her heels.

The phone rings.

– Mummy? Hello Mummy. I'm having my breakfast. Daddy made me my breakfast. Have you had your breakfast? Were the people at the conference strangers? Did you talk to strangers? Daddy took me to the swingpark and I spoke to a kid I didn't know. Are kids strangers?

– I'll explain later, okay? I have to speak to Dad.

– No, Mummy, explain now. Are you coming home soon, Mummy? Is this tomorrow?

– This is *today*. I'm coming home *today*.

# Red Tides

– But you said you were coming home tomorrow!

The mother draws in and holds her breath, counting, clenching her fists, holding back her breath, her disappointment, gripping the phone, not speaking until she has dragged her voice down from its inner scream, not speaking until slowly, softly, with deliberation, with a raging love she says:

– It's okay. I'll be home soon. This is tomorrow.

# Friendly Voices

– I have been here too long. The city has shrunk into a village. Incestuous is a word bandied about the place by the stretching web of people I know. Not that I have a wide circle of friends – I have never been especially liberal with my affections and intimacy is something for which I have always had a certain reserve. Incestuous is not an exact description but close enough. Unwholesome enough. Yet we are not people who wish to be associated with the dirty underside of life, the margins of existence, the underdog, subculture. We talk about it, of course, we are all too aware of our tenuous position and ambiguous relationship and sympathise with those who, through no fault of their own, have found themselves on the fraying edge of our society.

– It's the dug. Feart for it. Doesny say, like, but Raj knows well enough. Raj can smell the fear on her. Dirty big bastard that he is, makes straight for the crotch, pokes his wet nose into her baggy jeans. Ah let him sniff about a bit until she starts to get panicky, then ah call him aff and slap his arse so the both of them know who's boss around here. But ah'm an animal lover, a big softy where Raj is concerned. Love me love ma dug.

# Red Tides

*

– We talk about it, about them but keep our distance. We have created areas of safety for ourselves or at least put in speak-entry systems and requested unlisted telephone numbers from British Telecom. We take certain routes through the city, avoid others. We know well enough what those other routes are like. We've seen them all before; in our student days when everything was briefly, falsely equal and later, as young professionals, early in our careers when we preached and practised a hands-on approach. Grass roots. We got down to grass roots. Not that grass was a particularly common feature of the landscape.

– Once Raj has settled at my feet, the doctor crosses her legs and clutches the top knee. Funny, never seen the wummin in a skirt. Probably a policy no tae send them up here showing a leg, in case us lot, us *animals* get funny. Funny peculiar but. No supposed tae come up here on her ain, anyway, supposed tae have a mate wi her, for protection like. Ah tellt her she should get a dug of her ain. Hours of fun and guaranteed tae keep trouble at bay. That's unless trouble's got a dug of its ain.

– There's no need to be reminded. It doesn't do any good to be reminded of things we can't change. We're not heartless but practical, having learned from experience that we can only function efficiently by maintaining a certain distance. We have our own problems – who doesn't – but we are, at heart, solvers, not sinkers.

– When she comes in, she gies out this big sigh, like she's been holdin her breath all the way up in the lift. Probably has because the lift stinks. No all the time, no every single day. You might be lucky and catch it just after it's been washed, in which case you just about choke on the disinfectant. Me, ah'm used tae it. Doesnae mean ah like it, but some things you just put up wi.

Anyway, after Raj has had his wee thrill, ah let her settle intae the comfy chair and look around. She checks tae see how ah'm keeping the place, see if she can find clues as tae how the medication's workin afore she starts asking questions. No daft, this one, knows fine I'm a bloody liar, knows I'll say the first thing that comes intae ma heid tae confuse her. Tries tae get an idea of her ain, tae read between the fuckin lies ah spin her.

Shouldny come up here by hersel. Tryin tae make out she's brave and that, but she's crappin it all the same. She's all edgy, hingin aff the chair an that, eyes poppin out, kinda glaikit like, crossin the legs one way an the other. Her jeans rub thegither at the crotch and the denim makes a kinda scrapin sound. She gies a wee kid-on cough and pretends to be dead interested in ma latest picture a Christ on the Cross. Crucified in a field full a sheep. Quite pleased wi that one when ah done it but now ah'm nae sure. Ah've got hunners a crucifixions anyway. She looks at ma picture and ah look at her crotch. The dug has left a damp patch on her jeans.

– We've looked over the edge, know what lies there. We keep ourselves under control, in check, watch out for the signs, of losing the place, letting things slip. We know what to look out for. We're trained to spot the signs, like the weatherman is trained to read the clouds. It's what we do; spot the signs, make a forecast, though we like to think that the meanings are not fixed, that there are options involved, possibilities.

– No ma type at all, very plain. Nae make-up, jewellery – bet she's got plenty jewellery but leaves it at hame in case somebody gies her a doin – cropped hair, wee tits – ah mean, no a lot going for her, tae ma mind. Money but, she'll have plenty a that, plenty dosh for putting hersel out for the likes a me. Nice car. Nifty wee two-seater. Seen it last time she came. Frae the windae. Pale blue convertible. Can just picture her on a sunny day – the sleeveless dress on, something loose and cool, the open-toed sandals – pulling down the hood and belting out tae Loch Lomond. Bet she's a fast driver. Bet she gets a buzz frae rammin the accelerator intae the flair. Wouldnae mind a whirl in her motor masel. All ah ever get's the fucking ambulance or, for a treat, the paddy wagon. Ah'm no complainin but. Never say no tae a wee bit drama.

– Of course everything's relative. One only has to pick up the paper to be reminded just how much worse is daily life elsewhere: the Brazilian goldmine, say, where there is more malaria than gold; the bloody streets of Jerusalem or Johannesburg; the duplicitous back alleys of Bangkok or Rio; the hungry pavements of Bombay, New York, London. There are no goldmines on our doorstep, or war zones, no tin and board barrios, food queues. Yet.

– She gets the chat goin so she can start tae suss out the state a the hoose. Sometimes ah clean up for her comin, sometimes ah dinnae. Depends. The place is a pure tip the day. Even if ah'm feeling no bad ah sometimes let the mess lie anyway, just tae see how she takes it. Like tae keep her on her toes. Dinnae want tae make her job too easy for her. Thinks she can tell the state a ma heid frae whether I've washed the dishes or no. And the chat's all geared tae pick up clues. Thinks she can earn her dosh by droppin in for tea and chitchat. Tries tae guess how ah'm daein frae what videos ah've watched, what magazines ah've read. Ah like it when she gets on tae that. Ah get a chance tae use ma imagination. Make up some brilliant titles, all horror and porn. Ah like tae get a wee blush goin on her, see that pulse start up at her throat. It's no a lot a response but she's no meant tae respond at all. It's her job tae stay neutral.

She's no bad, but. Means well. Heart in the right place and all that guff. Wants tae help. Ah mean, she could've gone for one a they plum jobs in the private sector, analysin the rich and famous in some plush place down south. The nurse who comes tae gie me ma drugs, ma monthly jab, he tellt me she's top-notch, expert in her field. Could've been rakin it in, sinkin the excess intae a second hame, somewhere aff the beaten track, far away frae the hurly-burly a Harley Street, or wherever they doctors hing about these days. But no, she's chosen tae make her livin frae the likes a me.

– We complain, particularly about the larger issues, particularly on behalf of others. We are outraged about what is happening in the world, indeed the state of the globe is one of the most popular subjects for conversation amongst people like us. We lie awake at night and worry about the depletion of the ozone layer, preservatives in food, the destruction of the rain forest, the incidence of cancer near nuclear sites and the latest epidemics, about religious fundamentalism, neo-fascism, wars, riots, strikes, demonstrations, disasters natural and man-made – hurricanes, droughts and floods, about aphids, wild dogs and mad cows.

But we get up in the morning, the sun is shining, a scent of blossom is in the air, the grass is fresh and green beneath the litter and dog shit we are growing accustomed to in the municipal parks. Under a clear sky, joggers, dog-walkers, cyclists, down-

and-outs, students and parents of young children take the air together, at their own speeds. There are cycle lanes, walking lanes and jogging tracks. A bird sings. Blossom drifts in pink clouds above our heads. A man on a tractor cuts the grass and cleans up yesterday's mess. Another day passes without event, without people like us overstepping the boundary between the solvers and the sinkers. We have accumulated the life skills required to keep our individual globes turning fairly smoothly. We stay clear of the edge but don't allow ourselves to forget what lies beyond it. We care. People like us care.

– She's near drunk all her tea by the time she gets on tae the voices. Just about time for her tae get goin when she brings them up. Have they been friendly? she says. Eh? Your voices . . . she says. Aw aye. Have they been friendly? Aye, ah says, nae bother. Ah'm gonnae tell her about the state a ma heid, when the singin starts up. Ma ears go that plugged-up way like when you've got headphones on and the singin loups round ma heid. It's that kinda auld folky stuff, nae many words you can make out, just a miserable kinda moany sound but sorta nice wi it, soothin like. The doctor's askin me somethin. Ah cannae hear what she's saying, ah just know it's a question cos she's got her heid cocked tae the side, like a budgie. Raj is sittin at ma feet, lookin up at me wi big sad eyes, daft dug that he is. Sometimes ah think he hears ma voices tae. Ah gie him a clap and tickle his belly. Loves a good tickle, so he does.

– My office is bright, sunny. The walls are painted a pale, buttery yellow. On the wall facing the door is a small watercolour of a decorative plate and some pearly mussel shells. Behind my desk, above a shelf where I keep a constantly updated selection of leaflets (and my shade-loving ferns) is a calm abstract painting: Contemplation 4. There were three other remarkably similar paintings in the small gallery where I bought it. Any of them would have done just as well. Buying paintings is not a particular interest of mine. But I like those I have and they brighten up the office, give my patients (clients) something to look at while they try to untangle their troubles, sort them into words, order the chaos of their minds into sensible phrases. People don't like to look you in the eye when they tell you their troubles.

– It's no ma kind a singin but ah'm sittin here, hearin it, nae moving a muscle, an ah've got this amazin glow all over, ah'm feeling pure brilliant. Ah cannae explain it, ah've just got this kinda swellin in ma chest, like ma lungs is blowin up wi pure clean air, no the usual muck we suck in up this way. It's a gloomy auld tune, right enough, but it cheers me up no end. Here's this doctor, this consultant, sittin in ma chair, ma hoose, which may be a tip the day but isnae always. Next time she comes ah'm gonnae show her. Ah'll straighten it up, clean. Aye well sometimes it doesnae seem worth the bother just for me and the dug.

Just like me she is, this doctor, on her ain. Naebody tae cuddle in the night. Least ah've got the dug if ah'm desperate. What's she got? What does she snuggle up tae on a cauld night? A hot-water bottle, a teddy bear, a sex toy? Nae sae young neither tae be alane. Better get the skates on if she wants tae tie the knot. But then maybe she's one a they solitary types by choice, Christ. Or queer, aye that's a possibility. Ah mean she's no what ah'd call a man's wummin.

– Considering the design of the surgery, I'm fortunate to have a window. I've lined the sill with plants, the hardier varieties, those which require the minimum of attention. When I'm there, I play music, Vivaldi mostly, at low volume. I read somewhere about experiments on house plants to see how they reponded to different kinds of music. Rock music made the plants wilt whereas Vivaldi made them flourish and wrap themselves lovingly around the source of the music. I try to give people the same opportunity to flourish. I listen, offer tea, an old but comfortable armchair, now and then a sympathetic nod. Mostly I listen until my client has told me the first version. It's usually a slow, tiresome process, for both of us. I ask a few more questions and the client redrafts the problem.

I try to give people an opportunity to flourish but don't claim a high level of success. The nature of the task being what it is and nothing being absolute, even an accurate assessment is rarely possible. My plants do better, when I'm around to tend them, though I'm rarely in the office these days. In the catchment area served by our practice those who need me rarely come looking.

– It's that singing. Ah just get this overpowerin . . . ah just get this feeling that she could really dae wi a big hug. Ah get tae ma feet, cross the room and lift her aff her chair. Ah'm staunin there, huggin her, fair away wi masel till ah see the look in her eyes and Jesus fuckin Christ it's pure terror, the wummin's scared rigid, like a big cauld stane in ma hauns afore ah let go a her. And then the singing stops. Just like that. Like a tape being switched aff. Nae mair glow. That fuckin singin.

Doesny say anything about it, no a fuckin word. Just picks up her briefcase, tells me tae mind and be in for the nurse themorra, and goes. Raj chucks hissel at the door then slinks aff tae the kitchen. Needin fed but he'll have tae wait. Ah'm in nae mood for the fuckin dug. Ah hear her panicky wee steps as she hurries alang tae the lift. She'll no notice the stink on the way down, she'll be that happy just tae get the fuck out a here.

There she goes, marchin aff tae her motor, aff tae her next patient. Maybe she'll need a wee pit-stop somewhere, tae pull hersel thegither, get hersel nice and neutral again. When she's through wi us lot, put in her time, done her bit, she's gonnae nip back tae the surgery, tae her cheery wee office, take out ma file and bang in a new prescription. She's gonnae up the dosage, up it enough tae take away ma voices allthegither, blot them out, kill them aff. Didnae mean her any harm for fuck's sake, Christ ah was tryin tae be nice but she'll no see it that way, will she? She'll see it as a fuckin problem, and up the dosage. Tae bring me back tae ma senses, back tae The Real World. Tae this. The morra. Jab day themorra. Ah get the feelin ma voices areny gonnae be fuckin friendly the night.

# The Worst of It

He named his son Freedom because that was what he wanted for
him. The boy would wake when he was good and ready, wash, eat
and sleep according to nobody's schedule but his own, roam
wherever his childish fancy took him. He would have the horizon
at his fingertips. And, like his father, he'd go barefoot whenever
possible. Folks might not like it, those who reckoned that what
was needed in raising a boy was rules and training.

– Ain't no dog, Larry Myrtle would say, picking a strand of
tobacco out of his beard.

It was tough on Laura Jean, her husband's free-thinking. Laura
Jean liked things neat and tidy and nothing out of the ordinary,
nothing for folks to notice. Freedom ran about town barefoot and
unkempt, leaving in his wake a trail of disapproving glances. It
shouldn't be, people said, not in these modern times, there was no
need. When the boy gashed his toe on a broken bottle and spilled
blood all along the sidewalk, a storekeeper, who didn't give his
name, called up welfare and reported Freedom's shoeless
roamings to the authorities.

The following week a stiff-backed, skinny young man appeared
at Larry's door, dressed in a pale blue suit and black, shiny shoes.

# Red Tides

It was a hot spring morning. The young man's feet were damp and swollen. His shoes pinched. He was kept standing on the gravel path by the father while he related the complaint. He tried to see past the bearded, barefoot man picking his teeth with a penknife, but Larry – if his feet weren't in motion – had the habit of swaying from side to side, and what with the heat, the glare and all, the welfare worker didn't get a chance to check out the interior.

– You folks down at county buildings, you think wildness and badness is the same thing, s'that what you're tellin me?

– Didn't say that, sir.

– Didn't say you did, boy. Just doing a little personal surmising.

– Going barefoot is a health hazard, Mr Myrtle, sir.

– Somebody say my boy sick?

– Said he'd cut his foot and been bleeding all over the joint.

The young man scratched the bristly back of his neck, looked down at his pointy-toed shoes.

– Guess you wanna see him.

– Guess I do, sir.

Larry turned on his heels and called on the boy, who charged through the hall, butted his father in the gut, straightened up, grinned briefly, and held out a grubby hand to the welfare worker.

– Howdy, said the boy, and shook the stranger's hand gravely.

Since he was tiny Freedom had never been keen on scissors anywhere near his hair so he'd got to grow it long, like a girl's, got to keep his tumble of blonde curls, even though Larry knew – he'd seen with his own eyes – what happened to faggots, hippies, niggers, newcomers and anyone else who didn't qualify, whose face didn't fit. It wasn't pretty but then not too much about the town was pretty, except the view of the ocean. But the boy was still young, there was time enough to cut his hair.

Freedom stood on the stoop. His eyes – the same fierce blue as his mother's – narrowed into glittering slits against the sunlight. He was wearing nothing but a pair of loose canvas shorts, streaked, like his legs, with dirt. His skin was brown as a peanut, his slight body hard and muscular, more like the build of a healthy adolescent than a six-year-old. His teeth were strong, white and even, his toes long and straight. The welfare worker could see no sign of a festering wound.

– Y'oughta give up them things, said the boy, pointing at the young man's shoes. Leastways when it's hot. Them things is pure wicked to toes. He wiggled his own toes, making them tap out a rhythm on the planks, then sprung on to his hands, throwing his legs above his head.

The sun was beating down on the welfare worker's neck which was reddening above his collar. Nobody was inviting him into the shade of the porch. It must be near lunchtime. He was hungry. His schedule for the day was tight. It didn't look like he was going to get a damn thing settled here. He was ready to go. He'd put in a preliminary report and send out a letter.

Laura Jean came round the side of the house and picked her way across the gravel. She was wearing dark glasses, a skimpy white sun-dress and red, high-heeled sandals. She stopped on the driveway.

– Sellin somethin? she said to the welfare worker.

– No ma'am, he replied.

– Bible boy?

– Nope.

– Look like a bible boy to me.

Her mouth was smiling but the welfare worker couldn't see her eyes, couldn't see if they were smiling too. He wanted to see her eyes. He wanted to know what they were doing. He'd had a tough morning and this woman was a change from the lank-haired, slack-bodied, foul-mouthed mothers he'd called on earlier. She took a couple of steps towards him and he watched her hips sway, just a fraction, just enough.

The welfare worker pushed up the cuff of his jacket, pulling the shirt with it, exposing the watch.

– Well, I guess, he said, raising his clipboard to his chest like a shield, Better be getting along now. Be seeing you, Mr Myrtle, sir.

– The hell you will, boy, said Larry, as the welfare worker crunched down the drive to his car.

Larry had lived in town all his life but apart from Laura Jean and the boy, he paid it scant attention, took no part in its activities. The boat was what he gave his attention to. On the boat he felt real, whole, in control. He'd breathe in and feel the air hit the base of his lungs, taste the weather on his tongue, feel the heat or chill on his eyelids, the wind on the wings of his ears, on his spit-wet finger. He'd hunt the fish like someone possessed, dropping nets round the clock, go four, five, six nights without sleep, with nothing to keep him going but strong sweet coffee, candy bars and Willie Nelson crooning and crackling. Without making mistakes. Sometimes his eyes closed at the wheel and sometimes he saw things that weren't really there but he and the ocean got along.

He and the ocean had a fine arrangement, as relationships go, plenty of variety, a fair- and foul-weather romance. He loved her from his scalp to his toes, with their yellowed horny nails, toes which would stretch and spread on board and curl up on shore. Like his mind. His mind and his toes were very similar, if you were looking for connections; if you were the kind of person who needed to make connections. If you were like Larry Myrtle. When he was thinking, his toes responded. He could gauge the weather in his mind through his feet. It was a pity people didn't like him walking into bars and restaurants barefoot, but the God's honest truth was that his feet weren't too good to look at, and even though he always ordered the chef's special and tipped excessively, he was rarely made welcome.

It was the only real physical difference that he noticed, the curling and uncurling of his toes. Of course he rocked around like anyone else after a long sea trip and fell out of bed on his first night ashore, unless he slept out back in the hammock. Laura Jean had never taken kindly to this, in fact, she got kind of cold and quiet and hard inside when he picked up his sleeping bag from the woodshed, kissed her cheek and wandered outside to sleep under the stars, to be where he felt at home.

The house was confusing. It wasn't big – though room enough to satisfy Laura Jean – but it had too many doors. Sometimes he felt lost in his own home and called on Freedom to help him out. Mom's gone and changed things around again, one of them would say, although what was different wasn't easy to tell. Laura Jean kept the place like a showpiece in the mall. Unless she was mad at him and then she let it go right to hell. Thing was, only Laura Jean could give a damn about mess. The boy enjoyed the change of scenery, incorporated the household jumble into his games. Larry couldn't care less about the house. But he did care about Laura Jean, cared deeply and with an intensity which alarmed and saddened him.

They'd met up north. He'd been fishing off the New England coast for the summer. When the boat was docked – to unload the catch and stock up for the next trip – Larry and the rest of the crew slept on board and ate in town. After so much time cooped up together, the men liked to get off on their own. She'd been waitressing in a diner – Utility Lunch the place was called, a cheap, clean place which lived up to its name and didn't give itself no fancy airs. Larry's habit was never to eat at the same place twice but he broke it to sit and watch the tall, even-featured girl waiting on tables at Utility Lunch. It was the way she moved across the floor that he noticed first. Even when she was carrying a tray she walked straight and easy, unhurried, her feet noiselessly skimming the floor. Grace was what came to mind. Fluid grace.

It was soothing to watch her, like someone was massaging his eyelids, easing away the sting from too much looking and too little sleeping. Just sitting there was good, watching her moving back and forth. Better than hunting women in the bars. He drank more coffee than was good for him so he could hang out a bit longer, so she would bend over his table and pour the coffee into his cup, so he could hear her giggle lightly as the steam flushed up into her face, so he could smell her and look at her face up close. She smelled of honeysuckle and hamburger and coffee. Her eyes were bright and clear, her hair a downy blonde which looked natural. She didn't use much make-up, only a touch of pink on her lips, and a little dark stuff round the eyes, just enough to set off the blue of them.

Sometimes he still had the feeling that if he closed his eyes, if he stopped watching over Laura Jean, she'd vanish. They didn't make much sense as man and wife. Everything about Laura Jean was careful, refined, and smooth. She took great care of her appearance even though she didn't go anyplace much. She showered twice a day, waxed her legs religiously, pressed her clothes until they were sharp and crisp. And spotless. She might let the house go, but never herself.

Offshore Larry caught more fish than any of the other local skippers and it was all for her and the boy, to make them more comfortable. At home he worked his guts out to be a good husband, never let himself go overboard on booze or drugs, fixed what needed fixing about the house and spent all his free time with the boy. But no way could he look smart. He hated a razor and a buttoned-up collar more than most things, more than the way people squinted at his toes and his long, pointed teeth, more than walking down the hot street in sunshine and hearing spurts of laughter at his back – dirty, filthy laughter, his wife's name spat amongst all that filth. But they were only bored boys with nothing better to do and maybe he'd been the same. He couldn't remember. He didn't remember much about his boyhood. He didn't remember much about then. He'd made himself forget it, scrubbed at the memory until it had come up clean and raw, like a deck, empty and chafing and ready for the next catch.

He was a good husband but he was never what Laura Jean would have wanted, if she'd really sat down and thought about it. He didn't look right. He didn't speak right and he didn't speak enough. Laura Jean liked company. He was away more than home and when he was home he didn't say a whole lot. But the worst of it was how much he loved her. He loved her so much he was in constant fear of losing her, of pushing her away by some wrong move, word, look. His love for her made him frightened to go near her. At sea he imagined them together in every possible way but when it came to the real thing, to seeing her lying between crisp white sheets all grace and smoothness, the nearness, the scent of real warm flesh made him panic, clutch her roughly, press hard against her, inside her, fuck her in an ugly, terrified frenzy. Afterwards he felt like a criminal.

Laura Jean reapplied her lipstick, combed her hair, threw a light jacket over her sun-dress and picked up the car keys. Larry was sitting at the table, scratching out his list of supplies in his cramped, childish hand, the letters rocking and rolling across the page. His toes were in knots. A complete list was important. A simple omission, like salt or sugar or cigarettes, could make for serious problems. Meals, sleep and porn were the only diversions available. A good dinner counted for a lot, made all the difference, was something to look forward to and something to keep you going. He'd never taken drink on board, not since Billy Boy went over the side and got sliced in two. He didn't bother with the porn. It was for the crew. Single boys, mostly. They got kinda restless.

Because of the time of year, late spring, he was heading up north again, staying as long as there were fish to catch, which might be most of the summer. Since he'd become a family man, since he had Laura Jean and the boy to miss, to pine for, the summer fishing was something he dreaded, something he worked himself to the bone to get over with as fast as possible.

Last year his entire crew walked out on him after only two trips. He just pushed them – and himself, more than anyone – too damn hard, pushed the boys – and they were good boys too, that was the truth – to the point where they held out against him, told him to shove his catch, put his life on hold, told him he was turning into a crazy person, a goddamn mad Ahab and they wouldn't work for no crazy person, wouldn't drive themselves to an early grave. Big enough bucks were made taking things a mite more easy. Larry knew it, knew he asked too much. But every day away from Laura Jean pained him so much he couldn't, wouldn't slow up for fear another day would be what did it, what took her from him.

- How many days now? said the boy, pulling on Larry's arm.
- Three more breakfasts, said Larry.
- Wanna come, dad.

Larry looked up from his list and ran a rough, chapped hand through the boy's curls.

- So who's gonna look after Laura Jean for Larry Myrtle if it ain't Freedom?
- I guess. Guess I can take care of it.

As they drove downtown, Laura Jean began asking about the welfare worker. Mostly she was trying to figure out who had called him about the boy, like it would be better to know, to know where she stood, to know which stores to avoid. It wasn't so easy for Laura Jean to shut off from the talk. She had to live with it, after all. She was there living with it every day he wasn't around. He didn't know a whole lot about who she spent time with. She'd mention a few girlfriends, mothers she met for coffee or beer or cook-outs with the kids. But no men, she never mentioned men.

When Larry first met Laura Jean, she had a real low opinion of men. He couldn't quite figure it out. It seemed like he'd got her on his side because he'd been so hooked he'd asked for nothing, nothing at all. For sure that was how things worked out between them, when he asked for nothing. But now it was different, now he couldn't keep things clear in his head.

Out on the open water, he'd be standing at the wheel, watching the sway and swell of the waves, the sunlight leaping on the tips like flames. Fire on water. Flames which did not burn, did not consume. The ocean would not be consumed, would always be in motion. And constant motion was like a gentle hand across his face – smooth, light fingers stroking his eyelids.

It couldn't be enough for a girl like Laura Jean, on her own with the boy for weeks on end. The girl liked company and got precious little of it. He had the crew at least, day and night. Somebody to yell at across the deck. Didn't get down to much of a conversation but a few words here and there had always been enough for him. When the boy went to bed at night didn't Laura Jean feel lonesome? Didn't she ache to get out, to go running down the driveway in her high heels, in the dark, over the gravel, to something, somebody, somebody who didn't seize up at the sight of her and grip her arm on the street so hard his fingers left bruises? He couldn't see how she wasn't eaten up with restlessness, couldn't see how nobody wouldn't come by offering some personal consolation.

As usual, the days before sailing raced by in a flurry of preparations and leave-takings. Larry was about to try and fix some problem with the bathroom door that Laura Jean had just remembered about and couldn't wait all summer, when the phone rang. Laura Jean took the call. Larry was out in the shed picking up his tools. He went looking for Laura Jean to find out the exact problem and saw her talking on the phone, one foot resting against the wall.

Ten minutes later he came back again and found her still talking. She had a glass of red wine in her hand, the receiver cradled against her ear, head thrown back so he could see her throat, see the wine going down and the laughter bubbling up. And it seemed to him that it was the first time he'd heard her laugh since way back when she poured him all those cups of coffee in Utility Lunch. She still smiled a lot, she had an easy, open smile; but laugh? It sounded strange, different from the light, girlish laugh he had been so taken by. It sounded dirty.

– Gonna be all night? he said. Laura Jean mouthed something and waved him away.

By the time they sat down to eat, the pie crust was charred and the vegetables were soggy. Freedom had taken himself off to bed after bullying a promise out of Larry that next summer or for damn sure the summer after, they'd rent a place in New England. Laura Jean and the boy would drive up and spend the summer in port. And fishing. Next summer or the one after for sure the boy would get to go fishing.

They ate without speaking. Larry looked up from his plate at Laura Jean. Laura Jean was looking out of the window. Her mouth was open slightly, her lips moist and stained purple from the wine. The clock on the dresser had a loud, angry tick. Had it always sounded like that? How come he'd never noticed it before? In a couple of hours he'd have to sleep, to put in some hours of rest but now, now he had to get through to Laura Jean, he had to speak to her, had to stop listening to the time ticking away, to his heart racing, had to get across the ocean of silence welling up between them, reach across the table, cut through . . .

– Laura Jean . . . Honey . . . Something happening out there? Laura Jean turned away from the window.

– Couldn't you use a damn toothpick like any other person? Larry put the knife down on the table.

– Who called on phone?

– That welfare boy.

– I was telling Freedom we could rent a house up north next summer. You reckon?

Laura Jean looked down at her sandal dangling from her tanned foot. Her toenails were scarlet.

– Honey . . .

– You know I hate that name, Larry Myrtle, so why in God's
name d'ya havta keep on using it?

The clock again. The tick, the tap of Laura Jean's sandal against
the table-leg, the clockhand turning one two three circles, a late
bird twittering home to roost, the tightness in his chest, the
scratching of his toenails against his ankle.

– Chrissakes Larry, d'ya havta be such a goddamn peasant?
She looked straight at him, eyes flashing, no trace of a smile
anywhere. She'd said these exact same words before, but with a
smile, a kiss on the ear. Laura Jean had always preferred his ear
to his mouth. His mouth was kinda hard to get near, buried in
all that beard.

– Didn't never seem like it bothered you before.
– Maybe you just didn't notice, Larry Myrtle. Maybe there's a
whole lot you didn't notice.
– Like what?
– Like nothing.

Larry poured wine into Laura Jean's glass and then his own. He
raised his glass to his mouth and drank. And drank. Laura Jean
sipped and smoked and looked past him out of the window where
the darkness was seeping across the glass.

– Bathroom door's all fixed. Gonna havta tell Freedom to go
easy on them fixtures.
– Tell him yourself. He don't pay me no heed. Boy's gettin too
big and strong and wild for all this do-as-you-please, Larry.

# The Worst of It

– That what your welfare boy been saying?
– Maybe. Maybe I just figured it for myself.

Here in the house, with nothing moving except time, with the table solid and still, anchored between them, that was what it was, the lack of movement, that was all it was, if the house were rocking he'd know where he was, what to do, but as it was he was always off-balance, always needing to right himself, to square himself up.

– So what's the story with the welfare boy?
– What d'ya think? Shoes for the boy. A haircut. Schoolin.
– Took him a hell of a time to tell you that.
–
– Got a hankering for him, have you?
– Chrissakes, Larry. He was calling about *our son*.

Laura Jean stood up and began to clear the table. Larry watched as, with the old professional flair, she stacked the plates on her arm and moved to and fro between the sink and the table with the same fluid grace. But no smile. She splayed her fingers and scooped up the empty wine glasses. Larry caught hold of her, pulled her to him and pressed his face into the dark cloth of her blouse. He rocked against her, tried to picture her pouring coffee and smiling up at him through the steam. But he couldn't hold the picture in his mind, couldn't hold it against the sight of her talking on the phone to the welfare worker.

\*

The first catch of the season swings up from the stern. The

crammed, seething bag hangs over the deck while the gates are hooked. The line released, the net opened, the deck is knee-deep with the spoils of the sea. No matter how many times Larry goes hunting fish he's always disgusted by the first sight of the catch. Like something out of hell it was, an orgy of thrashing, flailing, gorging, a whole mess of sea life a-slipping and a-sliding every which way, eating, being eaten and all the while suffocating. Heads in mouths, tails in mouths, guts spilling through gills, egg sacs bursting and being swallowed up by the nearest free set of jaws.

The boys are already busy with their staves, spearing trash fish and kicking them through the slips. Larry wades into the thick of the catch to check it out. Too many frigging skate. One has sunk its teeth into his boot – a big one, belly up. He hates skate. Their sleek, grey backs he could cope with but belly up they were like an accusation: those pale undersides, the shocked, pink, throbbing mouths, the soft exposed genitals . . . The goddamn deck is covered in pale kite-shaped skate, covered in accusations.

The wound where his stave went in is oozing dark blood but the fish won't let go its grip of his boot. With his free foot Larry kicks at its head. The skate slaps, twists, hangs on. Larry raises his stave and brings it down again, this time between the eyes. The jaw jerks open. He yanks his boot free, sluices through the blood and guts and slime, trying to fix his mind on cod and flounder but all he sees are splayed white bellies, pink mouths, soft, defenceless skate. If he could just fix his mind on water, motion, the harmony of the waves, things might settle, he'd maybe get back his balance, the air could clear. But in his mind is fog and deep water and there's no way of telling.

# Cheap Shoes

Charlie T'Ang had most of his face immersed in a mess of ripe mango. It was one of his greatest pleasures. His eyes were closed as if to better taste the sweet juice dribbling on to his chin, his earlobes. With his eyes closed, in his mind he could be anywhere but mostly he stayed where he was, at his favourite table in his own restaurant, with his mango. It was quite enough excitement for a man of his age.

His son Bob sat in the glass-walled office, a conspicuous box which sat half-way between ground floor and first. Between heaven and hell, the house joke went, because of the contrast between the hectic, grubby chop-suey joint downstairs and the tranquil elegance of the Kumquat Room above. Bob was at his look-out post. It was close to five o'clock, when the shifts changed, and Bob liked to make sure the staff arrived on time. Charlie knew he was there, spying on him too, his eyes black needles of resentment. Everybody knew that the only way Charlie was going to hand over the business was by giving up the ghost, crossing the water, kicking the bucket. Charlie growled. Why did he have to remember that?

He slurped down the last of his consolatory mango then let

Cheng clean him up. Thoroughly and efficiently, his five-year-old great-granddaughter wiped his face and hands with a scented washcloth, told him off for making such a mess of himself and helped him to his feet. It was Happy Hour and at Happy Hour Cheng and Charlie handed out free chicken wings to any children they found in the restaurant. That was their job and both liked it fine. Charlie shuffled towards the kitchen. Cheng skipped ahead then turned to wait for him. Her great-grandfather was walking funny, like a duck. Cheng pointed at Charlie's feet and screeched with laughter.

– Charlie! You've got your shoes on the wrong feet!

– Pfff, said Charlie, without looking down. Cheap shoes.

# Glancing

Rain glances off shiny pavings at a crazy angle, wind slashes her face, her city clothes useless against the unrestrained elements of this wild, exposed island; she should turn back, make a dash for the green door with its B & B sign swaying above it, take the steep narrow stairs two at a time to her tasteful, verging-on-twee accommodation, strip off the wet clothes, snuggle up and listen to the racket the rain makes on the roof and the sea makes on the window, try and get used to it so it doesn't keep her awake like it did the night before. But she's been in the room enough, too much, and the solitude hasn't been soothing, in spite of bland little abstract collages on the walls, perky pot plants, an efficient heater, a sea view.

The people she's come out to meet haven't arrived yet and the place is so dreary it would have been funny, had there been anybody to share the joke with. Six lone lads hunch on bar-stools and mutter curses. At home, it's the kind of place she'd walk into and out of again and feel relieved to be standing in the rain. But she's here to meet people more prone to the animated huddle than the lonely line – and who should arrive shortly – so she buys a drink and takes it to the table facing a dormant juke-box. Even silent, the juke-box is better than nothing: modern, hundreds of songs to flip through, the casing dayglo pink and yellow; as out of place here as happiness. A deserted pool-table fills the back room. Above it, a lamp with a fringed shade casts a thin, smoky beam across the baize. The wallpaper is a repeat pattern of interlocking coffins.

She didn't think to bring anything to read, so reads the bar, which has been hammered together from fish-crates: ABERDEEN, WICK, THURSO, 2 doz COD 2 doz. WHITING. Reading the bar involves craning her head sideways and attracts attention. One of the boys at the bar glances round, his head swivelling slowly from the neck. Surreptitious. Reptilian. She concentrates on not meeting his eyes. To do this without obviously looking away, and maybe setting up some unspoken game of chase, she stares at the gap between him and his neighbour.

Her purse is heavy with coins, the juke-box enticing. She leaves her seat, feeds in a handful of change and begins to read the song titles, taking her time, reading slowly, re-reading, becoming deliberately engrossed in the business of choosing, flicking the card index forward and back again, making a pastime of indecision.

She must have pressed the wrong buttons. The juke-box plays nothing she chose, though the selection it thumps out could have been worse. The element of surprise is a distraction. The volume alone improves the place, for her if not for the others. It's good to be filling the dull air with the illusion of somewhere else.

She doesn't blame the locals for being gloomy. The day has gone from sodden grey to bruised blue. Who'd fancy the prospect of darkness for months on end? In a place like this, an island off the scrag end of the country, weather matters, makes a difference. There's a lot of it about, and when the sky's bright enough to see anything at all you see the weather coming. Rain clouds wheel, snow flurries shear over the hills, greybacks wail across this exposed, battered island and there's nothing to be done but stick it out.

Her drink's nearly done. She's going off the prospect of meeting people. Friends of friends. Theatre people on tour. Nothing to do with her. She could go now, skip out and miss them. She's come all the way here for peace and quiet, after all. Many do, in summer, and clutter up the narrow streets. Off season, she's one of a handful of visitors. The tourist shops are deserted or closed. What she'd wanted. But peace and quiet haven't been having the desired effect, the juke-box is still playing and she hasn't had her money's worth yet.

The lad with the lank, sandy fringe is getting bold, letting his eyes linger, willing her to look at him, to adjust the angles of her eyes just a fraction, and meet his. Eye contact, coinciding lines of vision, that's the game, but she's not playing. After two more random selections and several failed attempts to catch her eye, he cracks down his glass, scowls in her direction and lurches out into the rain. Behind him the door bangs, predictably.

Another lad strolls over to the juke-box. Smallish, dark tidy hair, white shirt, denims. The disc drops, clicks into place, makes a couple of scratchy revolutions. A piano mourns, brushes drag over a drum, lead in to Joe Cocker's melancholy squeal:

*I looked out over nowhere, there was nothing at all . . .*

– I like this one, he says.

He shifts his hips to a couple of bars then turns to face her. A pinkish baby face, squint smile, bright eyes. Clean-cut. Fresh-faced.

She liked the song too. Hadn't chosen it. A song for the lonely, the heartbroken, and she wasn't that.

– Come and play pool, he says. It'll cheer you up.

She makes excuses to stay put – doesn't need cheered up, wants to hear the music, can't play pool – but he's persistent and points out, in a light, easy way that she can do what she's doing, feel what she's feeling and still knock some balls across the table.

He chalks cues. Big smile.

– What's your name?

– Joanne.

– And where're ye frae, Joanne?

– Edinburgh.

– Edinburgh, eh? Ah've a half-brother doon there. Muirhoose. And whit're ye daein here?

– Getting away from Edinburgh.

He draws in his breath, lines up his cue, fires at the racked balls, sends them rocketing across the table.

– And whit're ye daein in the pub? Ah'm nosey by the way.

– Having a drink and playing pool.

Big smile again. Shirt-sleeves pushed up to the elbow.

– Aye, ah ken. But aboot here lassies dinna come intae pubs on their ain.

– I'm meeting people.

– Local folk?

– City people. In a show at the town hall.

– Ach well.

He's got an appealing, wee-boy cheekiness about him, and dimples.

She hasn't played pool for years but begins to enjoy the game, the geometry, the way you could see one action causing another, the contrast between a direct hit and the knock-on effect of a duff shot. If you could lay your life on a table, work out the angles of contact, predict the knock-on effects . . . And circling the table fills time better than staring at the juke-box or the fish-crate bar.

– Ah'm a butcher, he says. Wis on the fishin but oot a work mair than in it. It's a job. Jimmy's in Muirhoose, like ah said. Except he's no there that much ah don't think. No that ah ken how he comes and goes. No seen him in five year. In the forces, like, been all over the place. Belfast. Falklands. The Gulf. In the paras now. A hero, he is. Medals and everything. Shot! Tch, and you said you couldna play!

– Cracked up one time. Lost the place he did. Hit the deck every time a bloody car backfired – thought it was gunshot, ken. And a pure mental temper he had, raging. Put a boy in hospital and himself in the cells. Better now, ken. Been asked to go into the flying squad, S.A.S., like.

He goes for hard shots, spinning out the game.

– If he goes for it, if he signs up, they give him this contract which says – ah'm no supposed tae ken this, top secret like – but if something happens to him, if he gets done in, all his faimily – mither, faither, wife, bairns – they'll all be taken care of. A pension, ken. And protection. No that he's got wife or bairns yet.

She's taking her time too, eyeing up possible angles. The dreary little backroom is warmed by the boy's soft island voice, easy smile, his ready confidences.

– No me, like. Half-bloods dinna coont. Last time ah saw him, ah wis in the shop – new tae the trade then but an auld hand noo – ah was standin at the coonter and this big laddie – a full six inches taller'n me – is standin on the ither side, sayin: 'Get a fuckin move on there, Alex,' – that's my name by the way – and ah'm thinking, How does this lad ken ma name? ah says to him, 'Do ah ken you?' And he says, 'You fucking should, you cunt. ah'm your fucking brother.'

– Excuse the language but you shoulda seen me. Stopped in ma tracks, rigid ah wis. The cleaver above ma heid and ma mooth wide open, like ah'd seen a bloody ghost. If there hadna been the pork chops and the big high coonter atween us ah'd have thrown ma airms roon him right there and then. When ah got off ma shift we came doon here, drank pints and pints, then staggered up the brae, huggin each other and greetin like bairns. Hadna seen each other since primary school.

He misses a shot. Still grinning, he points the tip of his cue at an easy ball.

– There you are. Ah'm giving you a chance . . . He hung aboot awhile, hiked over every incha the toon in his DMs – it was pissing rain the whole time he was here, like tonight. Liked the place, so he did; slagged it off, ken, but jokin like. He was a laugh. Ah miss him. Dinna really ken him, like, but ah miss him.

A lucky shot wins her the game. The remaining balls are returned to their pockets. Without their rolling geometry, the click of contact, the room resumes its usual dreariness.

– Are ye for another lager? he says, but she's ready to go, to get out before the theatre people arrive . . .

– Ach well. At least you're smiling now. When you came in, ken, you had a face like thunder.

The room is warm. She wraps a towel round her wet hair, pushes her toes into thick, dry socks, cups her hands around a mug of steaming tea. She'd missed the theatre people, after all, missed them on purpose. As she turned back along the street, she'd heard them straggling down the brae, their sharp city voices cutting through the island storm. Lowering her head into the rain, she'd kept on walking.

It is a good room. She was lucky to find such a good room. More home comforts than home, in some ways. Simple. A clean calm room in the midst of a storm. She wipes the condensation off the window, looks past crooked chimney stacks and sagging walls, looks through shifting masses of darkness towards the rain-streaked lighthouse beam way out in the bay.

# A Little Bit of Trust

It was almost dark. The heat had gone out of the day and Malek had sold no carpets. He pushed his hands deep into the pockets of his Italian coat, savouring is warmth, its style. Maybe he'd have to sell it. His fingers rubbed against the flaccid, greasy banknotes. Twenty dirham. Enough for something to eat but not enough for wine and wine was what he wanted, needed. Tourists were thin on the ground now and the few backpackers who drifted round town day after day were a waste of time, spinning out their cash and days like threads, eating bad food which made them sick, so they could hang out in the sun a bit longer.

Malek had sold no carpets though he'd been pacing the alley since early morning. Now it was almost dark and there was nothing to be done but wait and see if tomorrow brought in a busload of Germans. The way things were, the bad situation getting worse from one newsflash to another, the world rushing towards war, it was not at all likely that tomorrow would bring anything better than today.

Maybe he'd visit his mother after he closed up. She'd feed him. He'd get an earful of her worries about his bad ways but he'd still have money in his pocket. Yesterday Yousseff had sold a carpet, everybody knew it. It had taken him two hours, several pots of tea and a mountain of patience but he'd done it, he'd got rid of a carpet. Maybe Youseff could spare enough to make up the difference on a bottle.

Jane had been wandering the town for hours, trying to acquaint herself with the medina, to fix in her mind the maze of twisting alleys within the walls of the old town. In spite of assuming an air of determined confidence (as recommended in her guide book), in spite of having done this kind of thing before – in places where more overt hostility had greeted her, where the stares had been more accusing than curious, the swearing more vehement, the spitting more accurate, where worse horrors had swarmed in the shadows – still the place evaded her.

Every alley seemed the same, crammed with people and produce, the air heavy with smells – spice, petrol, perfume, drains, everywhere the jangle of horns, bells, cart-wheels, and radios blasting out a jarring mix of eastern and western music. So many people extended a hand – a beseeching, scabrous hand or firm insistent trader's hand – everyone saw her coming, her skin pale as a mushroom, her hair an ashy blonde. She stood out from these dark, forbidding people like an aberration.

Turning a corner and finding herself out of the medina at last, back on the main street not far from her hotel, looking up and seeing the clocktower black and solid against the last dregs of sunlight, Jane's eyes began to water. Perhaps it was the dust. There was a great deal of dust, of course, dry red dust, like the paprika and harissa which the spice merchants piled into fiery pyramids, the sky was thick with dust, the light a colloidal orange as the sun dropped behind the ramparts.

Jane's eyes hurt. They were tight, stinging around the rims, contracting in on themselves, shrinking into pinpoints. For several nights she had barely slept. She had gone beyond normal weariness into a fatigue which brought with it a surreal super-awareness, an ultra-sensitivity. Everything ached and clenched, from her bones to her guts to the pores of her skin. Her teeth ground together as she held a tense, pained smile. In addition to fatigue an indefinable sadness.

The muezzin's sunset call from the clocktower reminded Malek that drinking was bad for body and soul but Allah says everyone is free, and he would drink if he got the chance. Others did. Tourists came to town, ate in restaurants every night and drank in the waterfront bars until they couldn't walk and had a taxi take them a hundred metres to their hotel. Tourists could do what they wanted, no problem. All they had to do was pay; tourists in their designer clothes, haggling over the price of a carpet, happy only when they came away with a bargain, settling only for the cheapest price, never believing that when the vendor got down to his last price he'd sold for no profit, only for ready cash – because you can't eat carpets – tourists hiding their money as they counted it, as if the very walls of the medina were out to cheat them, tourists excited and happy, making a transaction, rolling up a carpet, imagining going home to their cold grey country with the bright beautiful thing, spreading it on the floor, pointing out aspects of the handiwork, urging friends to feel the quality. Later they would walk all over it in their dirty outdoor shoes until it was dull and threadbare, by which time they'd be thinking about another holiday in the sun, about living it up in a place where for them everything was cheap, dirt cheap, thinking about buying another carpet. Tourists – he wanted to piss on them all.

She had come for a rest and here she was, walking down the street
with tears springing from her eyes, keeping on walking because if
she stopped she would crack, right there in the middle of the
street, amongst dark, forbidding strangers. And if she cracked,
would she mend? She put on her sunglasses. Here women hid
their entire bodies beneath wraps and veils: all she could hide was
her eyes. But it was too dark for sunglasses. She could barely see.
She was bumping into people. The tears were already trickling
below the black plastic frames and spreading over her cheeks so
she removed the sunglasses, wiped her eyes and – seeing a pretty
courtyard draped with carpets – left the main street again.

He was just about to lift the carpets off the wall and take them
inside for the night when the woman came by. It was her jacket he
noticed first, a loose, shimmery black thing which picked up the
reflections from the coloured lights in the rubber tree. New to
town, he could tell. She walked slowly, only the blue eyes raced,
scanning walls and shop-windows. Nervous, he could tell.
Clutching her purse so hard her knuckles shone through her
white skin. She held herself straight, stiff, but when she turned to
watch as he unhooked a handsome silk kilim, her jacket rippled,
softening the angles of her body. Not French. Not German.

   – Hello! How are you? Welcome!
She looked at him, straight at him.
   – I like your jacket, he said, and – knowing the answer –
added, Did you buy it here, in Morocco?
   Of course she shook her head and at that moment he should
have asked her into the shop, offered tea, pulled out the carpets
but she was already past the door, he had been too slow, too taken
up with admiring her jacket, wondering what it cost, too busy

looking at her eyes, mouth, breasts, legs, and trying to think of something else to say in English. But his English was not so good, he was out of practice, so when he finally called: 'Come please. Only for look, no for buy,' it was too late.

The moment to embark on a sale had passed, the moment when their eyes had met. Now her back was to him, her long shimmering back, and she had to look over her shoulder, to reply, in English:

– Another time perhaps. I need to eat.


That's when he should have let her go and find the ugly overpriced hole she'd circled in her guide book but no, he'd taken hold of her arm – and she had put up only a little resistance – and guided her to Restaurant Yasmine.

– A clean place, not expensive, very near.

– Your brother's place, is it? she said, but not nastily, not like a smart-ass tourist, not that hard, knowing tone he had endured day after day before all this talk of war killed off business. He denied any connection to the patron of Yasmine; though, of course, Amal would slip him a couple of coins for bringing in a customer. With weary amusement she let him settle her at a table, summon the waiter, shake her hand as if being led around was all a harmless little game, no big rip-off.

– *Bon appétit*, he said, and went back to close up the shop.


She had gone past hunger. Eating was an effort. Her hand shook as she lifted forkfuls of spicy stew to her mouth. Though the restaurant was deserted, though there was no one to notice her except the waiter, she felt too visible, too conscious of every movement, as if she had lost the habit of eating. Food fell off her fork, stringy bits of meat and vegetables lodged between her teeth, her cutlery rattled against the hot clay bowl.

The commotion outside was a convenient distraction from the gravy-spattered tablecloth and the embossed wallpaper. A procession of some sort, announced by drums and demented pipes, passed the open door of the restaurant. From her seat she could see a long table being carried through the narrow alley, a table set with cloth, candlesticks, flowers and utensils, held aloft, rocking by on the swell of the crowd. A table and then a calf, skittering behind.

The wedding feast, on spindly legs, pissed with abandon as it was nudged towards its own slaughter. Malek hammered home the lock on the shop door. When he recognised the wedding party he spat loudly into the dust. The husband, an English with wispy hair and a belly like a woman with child, a forty-year-old English marrying a local girl, a virgin of sixteen years. He'd come here for that, lived half his life doing whatever with women and now he wanted to buy himself a child bride – and of course these poor people had given him their daughter – he wanted feasting and dancing, the *mariage typique*, the big ritual, he wanted his guests waiting outside the door so he could go to them with his bride's bikini briefs and say: 'See? I have made a woman from this girl. See, the blood of my wife.'

Jane put the change from the large bill into her wallet, left the restaurant and walked straight into the path of the man from the carpet shop who was approaching her. He was walking between a young man and woman. Their arms were linked. They were laughing. When he saw her he broke away from his friends.

– Did you enjoy your meal? You want to drink something?

– Where?

– Where you like.

He felt for the money in his pocket. A crisp fifty – thanks to his good luck of running into Youseff and Fatima – and twenty of his own.

Without thinking she had responded, without making any decisions Jane had begun to walk in step with Malek. His friends had gone.

– Not far, she said. I don't want to go far.

– Of course. You want to be near your hotel. I know this. No problem.

When the first bottle was empty he wanted to order another but she said:

– I'm tired. I should go now. Back to my hotel.

– No, please. Stay longer, just a little longer, he said, reaching for her hand which she withdrew.

– Please, he said, I like you, you understand? We drink one more bottle, then I take you to your hotel, no problem. Please, he said and when he spoke he seemed so sad, so hurt by her refusal, as if all he wanted was a little bit of trust, a little more time together, nothing else, no sex adventures, he knew her situation, knew she was not free, she had made her situation clear before they reached the bar. And it was better sitting there, drinking wine and looking out at the sea, better than huddling under too few blankets in the gloomy hotel room with its maroon curtains and dirty yellow walls.

– Please, because for me . . . you know what is *coup de foudre?*

She didn't. And she had left her dictionary in her hotel room. And his explanations involving a flash in the sky did not clarify anything. But when the waiter appeared with another bottle she remained seated and let her glass be refilled. When the wine ran low, so did his English and her French, and Arabic was out of the question. She took to looking out at the boats in the harbour, he to watching her. He could tell that in her mind she was far away from this place, this man she didn't know, in her mind she was on another shore, in another bar, with another man, her husband, an English, maybe like the one in town who'd be at that moment dancing with his Moroccan bride, preparing to penetrate her body and no questions asked. The family and the nation had given their permission, opened their arms and said, Come in. Welcome. Take what we offer. You can pay the price. It is a good price, special price for special person. Nothing to you.

She was looking out to sea and he was looking at her elegant jacket and the fat purse at her fingertips. How much did she have in there? And at home? A car, a video, hot water day and night, a wardrobe full of good clothes? The Italian coat was all he had and maybe he'd have to sell it. And what would she take home? What would she take from his country? It was always take with tourists. Souvenirs, photos, memories.

A carpet would look good in her house. Maybe she had a big house, maybe she'd take home two, three, four carpets, maybe he could really make a sale. If everything was nice for her tonight, maybe tomorrow she'd come to the shop, he'd serve her with tea and they'd make some good business, enough to keep him going for many weeks. But she hadn't said anything about buying a carpet. In fact, she'd said many times already that she had not come here to buy, that she did not want to buy, she hated bargaining, it was not her way. She was clear about that, about her way, definite, as if at other times – when she was not so tired and so far from home – her life was a neat and intricate pattern, one she had chosen from a whole range, the way she might choose a carpet.

– Your jacket is like the sea in moonlight, he said, touching her sleeve, but his pretty phrase didn't bring her eyes back to his and now that the wine had been drunk and paid for – he had offered to contribute Youssef's fifty but she refused it – now he should take her to her hotel.

The night air bites as they walk across the uneven cobbles of the harbour. Her jacket is thin. She is cold. Though she protests, he takes off his coat and drapes it over her shoulders. The waves can be heard smashing against the sea-wall. The boats creak and scrape together. Away from the bar the harbour is badly lit. No one is about.

– Come and hear the sea, he says, as they veer away from the exit towards the far side of the harbour.

– I can hear it, she says, and stops, but he is pressing her to go further, to give him just a little bit of trust, and just as she is thinking that it would be good to feel the spray on her face, that had she been in her own country she would have gone – accompanied or alone – past the dark huddle of boats to the sea-wall, just as she is beginning to feel sick of her own fear and suspicion – she has been saying No, No thank you, Another time perhaps, since she arrived – just as all this denial is getting to her, he grips her arms.

– Come please. You come now, please, he is saying but the tone has changed, the 'please' is no longer a polite request, he is pressing her towards the dark and she knows she has already taken a step too far, such a short step and yet everything has changed, the bar is already too far away, her hotel also . . .

*

. . . but how can she push him away now, she who'd sat all night asking questions about the crafts, the spices, the economy, the lives of girls and women, the *mariage typique*, the war, and he had told her everything he knew. It had not been easy for him to say so much in English and she had wanted details, wanted to take from him so many details, he had given and she had taken and now . . . He lets go of her. He needs to piss.

Moving away to the sound of his urine hissing over the cobbles, walking fast, she puts a distance between them. When she reaches the exit to the harbour, she begins to run across the lorry park. She remembers that she is still wearing his coat, she throws it off her shoulders, the ground is muddy, her shoes become caked in mud, the mud slows her down, her feet drag but she doesn't stop, with each step she is nearer her hotel. He picks up the coat. He continues to follow her but is too far behind to catch up, close enough only to wave his muddy coat in the air, to wave his coat like a flag and roar at her shimmering back:

– I hate you! You and your filthy rich nation! You understand!

# Barely an Incident

She ran into the station just in time to see the tail-lights of her train being sucked away into the dark throat of the tunnel. Above the shuttle platform, blue banners swayed in its wake, like drunks. More time to be put to no good use. It had been one of those days already, without missing the bloody train. The evening meeting had dragged itself to a close with nothing resolved, except where and when the next meeting would take place. It was part of the job, showing her face, putting in hours in the windowless meeting-room, as one after another suggestion was passed around like an unwanted parcel. If we get A from B and C comes up with D, if E is prepared to give F to G, and so on through the directory of funding bodies to be begged, flattered or bullied into parting with a chunk of their tightly clutched and hopelessly insufficient budget. The notepad with damn all on it but doodles and queries. Nothing but coffee and cigarettes since noon. She was a wide-awake zombie again.

The station was deserted and freezing, as only a station could be, icy draughts snaking in from all corners. Snow had fallen earlier, turning to sleet and finally rain. Wet dripped through holes in the roof, where neurotic city birds were twittering away, duped by round-the-clock lighting into believing it was day and time to sing. The lino-tiled concourse was slittered with coffee, beer and slush. In the far corner, a hunched woman was pushing a brush, eyeing the floor with contempt, as if there were no point in doing what would just have to be done all over again.

The station was bleak at the best of times and if you couldn't face the bar and its odour of weary, anonymous transience, there was nowhere to sit, except the dank Superloos or the slippery metal seating-rings, stuck out on the concourse like high-tech dough-nuts. Whoever designed those seats must have been convinced that the last thing a traveller wants is to be friendly. Folk fanned away from each other, like spokes on a wheel, points on a compass. A deliberate effort was required to catch your neighbour's eye.

Her hands were a blotchy tartan and burned. She couldn't feel her feet. Trails of melting sleet squirmed through her hair and dripped down the back of her neck. Time to kill but she wasn't going to pace to and fro like the commuting musician – there was always one around in this year of culture – clutching an instrument case to his chest, like a mummified lover. Nor was she going to peer at the small print on the posters advertising weekend breaks in Paris or Amsterdam. She'd seen them all before and anyway, they'd only make her restless or miserable or both. That was the trouble with stations – there was always a more tempting destination than your own.

It was too cold, exposed and lonely out on the doughnut seats so she stood in the entrance to the carry-out burger bar, where an overhead heater puffed out stingy clouds of warmth. She should eat, but one look at the blown-up photos of buns oozing melted cheese and sweaty beef and she was digging in her pockets for cigarettes. The news-stand, coffee bar and fruitbarrow were closed and barred for the night. If you really needed to spend money, you could still get passport photos from the curtained booth, business cards from the autoprinter, donate to city hospitals by dropping money into a Howitzer shell, or Test Your Emotional Temperature on The Passion Chart, if you were prepared to squeeze a couple of phallic handlebars. Nothing else to do but look at the clock, the Arrivals and Departures board – on which nothing was imminent – and the people.

Apart from a bag lady who was curled round one of the ring seats like a seal, asleep – or trying to be – the only people using the seats were a young couple, Japanese perhaps, or Malaysian, she couldn't tell, couldn't really see them clearly because three lads, lager cans in hand, had rocked to a halt in front of them, stamping their boots and splashing filth from the floor at the small, compact couple and their tidy bundle of belongings.

– Sorry, mate, one of them said, Ah mean ah'm really fucking sorry but.

He squinted at his can – it had a pin-up on the back – took a swig, tipped it so the dregs dribbled on to the girl's shoes, staggered back a couple of steps, steadied himself briefly, then reeled in the direction of the taxi rank. The other two were still standing over the pair on the seat. One of them bent down so his eyes were on a level with the boy, and inches away from his face.

– Heh heh – WHO FLUNG DUNG?

There was a flurry of movement on the seat, a flash of white shirt as the boy twisted to get a better grip of his girlfriend, jerking her towards him. With his free hand he pushed a blue-black lick of hair out of his eyes. His eyes batted from side to side as if they were on elastic.

– Ah said, WHO FLUNG DUNG?

– Don't know, said the boy. Sorry. Don't know.

His panicky vowels rolled around the empty station like skittles.

– That's a good one, eh Barry? Bastard disnae know.

– Does he no?

– No. Nothing like ignorance, eh?

– You put him right, man, put him in the picture.

– Ach, wouldnae waste ma breath.

The girl began to cry, quietly. She had her glasses off and was plugging up the tears with her fingertips but the shiny drops kept oozing through, breaking up and trailing down her cheeks like scars or wrinkles. The boy circled her with his arms, putting his body in front of hers like a shield or a blanket, as if by enveloping her he could mend the damage, make the tears stop. He was talking non-stop into her chest, rocking the girl against him.

– Ah'm starvin, man, so ah am.

– Fancy a chinky, eh? Deid cat chop suey. Hey – WHO FLUNG DUNG!

The automatic doors wheezed open and shut the three of them out, leaving behind the sour echo of their laughter. And just as they left, in walked a couple of the boys in blue. It was farcical – the timing was spot-on – but not funny. They were doing the rounds, a gangly one and an older, stockier one, strolling, chatting amiably. They were not looking around much, just glancing here and there, as if they didn't want to notice anything they might have to deal with, as if they were actually trying not to pay attention.

Should she report the incident, get the bastards booked? Names, addresses, questions, notes in the wee black book. It was provocation, no doubt about it. But it could have been worse, what might have happened could have been so much worse. No blood, wounds, no visible damage, nothing you could put a finger on, barely an incident and yet anger welled up in her – anger and hate. She wanted revenge, reprisals, wanted them dragged back and paraded through the square, chained at the neck, their tongues cut out and all the other atrocities race had committed on race. But mostly she wanted the girl to stop crying.

It was terrible, seeing the boy trying so hard to comfort the girl and getting nowhere, the pair of them a contorted huddle of distress, shipwrecked on the concourse. The boys in blue ignored them. The gangly one jerked a thumb at the bag lady humping about under her coat. The stocky one checked his watch and shrugged. They'd shift her later.

She was standing right where they had stood, in a puddle of spilt lager.
  – Excuse me.
  –
  – Excuse me but were those people bothering you?
  – Don't know, don't know!
The boy sprang up from the seat, fist raised, eyes flashing. She jumped back, expecting a blow, but the boy checked himself in mid-swing. The girl stared, open-mouthed and impassive. Up close she could see how young they were. Pimply kids in thin

clothes. First loves maybe. Wanting to draw a curtain on the world. But the world wouldn't be shut out, go away or mind its own business.

– Those people . . .
She pointed in the direction of the automatic doors. She hadn't even thought of what to say, just walked right up, intruded, forced herself on them.

– They're just drunk. Don't pay any attention. Please.

But that wasn't it. That wasn't what she'd meant to say at all, and she could hear the plaintive whine in her voice. The boy lowered his arm slowly, sat down and resumed his grip on the girl. She fiddled with her glasses, clicking the legs against the frames, lifting them to her eyes then, changing her mind, slamming them into her lap. What's it to you, her eyes demanded, What's it to you?

– You are very kind thank you for your trouble.
The boy's words rattled out, a memorised response, polite standby for any occasion.

– It's no trouble, she said, To me. It's you who had the trouble. Sorry, she said. I'm really sorry.

There was nothing more to say and she was getting uncomfortable and embarrassed by the whole thing. There was no sign of her train yet, so she walked back to her spot outside the burger bar and went on waiting, making a point of not looking in the direction of the seats. She was tired, of people, herself, of hate and stupidity, wasted time and missed connections, the weight of work in her bag, tired of being out.

Maybe the girl had been upset about something else, maybe they hadn't even understood the insult, maybe the two of them had been fighting, or somebody they knew was sick, or recently deceased. Maybe she'd failed an exam – they looked more like students than tourists – or lost her job, or even just been to see a film with a sad ending. What did she know? The girl could have been crying about all kinds of things.

As she hurried across the concourse towards the train pulling up on platform six, she glanced back. The girl was still crying. Her blundering spiel had done nothing to help. Maybe even made things worse. After all, when did anybody ever thank you for poking your nose in, interfering. And what she'd said – *those people* – what did she really know about them? And *just drunk*. Just? What kind of excuse was that? – Sorry, I don't know, don't remember, am not in control of what I'm doing because I've had too much to drink – The national excuse for everything, from bad-mouthing to murder. And she had gone along with it, just like everybody else.

# Street of the Three Terraces

There is a street in the city, a curving, high-standing terrace with some of the best views in the city. It is divided in three by name and outlook.

Section 1: north-facing. At a respectable distance – beyond a leafy embankment, fenced, and the wide straight London Road – grimy tenements sweep downhill to the newly renovated port where, in conjunction with cheap but not always cheerful pubs, warehouses and cut-price carpet shops, a clutch of smart restaurants have recently opened. Tourists and city people go to these new places, to eat, drink and soak up the local atmosphere. Looking out over the docks, where flat-hulled swans glide across oil slicks, they sip chilled white wine or real ale, and sample locally caught seafood, amongst darkly gleaming gantries, brass fittings and *objets d'art*. Outside is the atmosphere, bands of off-duty seamen and lorry-drivers, looking for bars, brawls, women. There is little interaction between the spectacle and the spectators.

Section 2: it is the back view, to the south, which catches the eye.

A huge, shared garden backs on to the The Hill, a prominent mound, famous for its observatory, monument to Nelson, pillared folly and its popularity as a gay rendezvous. In spite of its centrality, the hill is a lonely isolated place where the wind wolf-whistles through the tough grass and musses the carefully-groomed hair of solitary young men.

Section 3: turning away from that high spot in favour of another, facing east and eventually the sea, volcanic rock rises out of parkland. Some say the rock resembles a sleeping giant. From the terrace the view is best in winter, glimpsed through bare trees. In summer, foliage crowds out the view and the street becomes a fragrant retreat. The city's noise, dirt, deprivation is far enough beyond the scrubbed doorsteps to be out of earshot, sight, mind.

To live on the street costs a good deal of money. The four-storey houses are grand but – as many of their owners would take pains to tell you – monsters to keep up. Hotels, offices for professional bodies, art galleries (private, fine art only) and consulates have mostly replaced private dwellings and much of the remainder has been divided up into flats. American CIA men are reputed to jog by day in the shared back garden, in reality a park of several acres where nanny-tended children fight over non-violent toys. The terrace is discreet, aloof, undisturbed. Because it has little value as a thoroughfare, many people are unaware of its existence.

On a warm night in early summer, in the midst of chestnut blossom, rhododendrons and rogue bluebells, while an aria sung by Pavarotti drifted on to the terrace through an open window, a young man was beaten to death.

*

## Street of the Three Terraces

Words used by the press and media to describe the murder: brutal, vicious, depraved, horrific, fiendish, sadistic, merciless, mindless, motiveless. Words used by the police and the accused: poof-bashing.

The accused: Five teenage boys.

The weapons found in their possession: one machete (blunt), a length of studded rubber tubing, an iron bar, two craft knives. The Dr Martens boots which several boys wore were fitted with steel toecaps.

HOMOSEXUAL HAUNT MURDER: ACCUSED BLAME EACH OTHER: The victim, a stranger to the city, suffered multiple injuries before he died, including what appeared to be an attempted castration. It was said that the assault continued even after the victim had been beaten unconscious and left hanging upside down with his trouser leg caught on a railing. When it was suggested by one of the accused that an ambulance be called, one of the boys, who cannot be named for legal reasons, refused and went on to 'finish him off'. All five boys deny the murder. All five have also lodged a special defence of incrimination, naming the others accused.

Across the London Road and a few blocks down the hill from the terrace, on the fourth floor of a blackened tenement which has been awaiting renovation under an urban restoration project for ten years, live the family of one of the accused, Billy McBain: his mother, Bet, father Joe, sister Noreen.

– I'm no saying he was an angel or nothing, and Joe and me've been through our share of trouble with the boy. But nothing no other lad his age wouldn't get up to, no nothing over the score, nothing anywhere near this. It can't be right. He tells me – and I have to believe him – I just have to, see, he's my son and I'm his ma and blood's thicker than water, right? Says he was there all right, wi his pals. But no, they weren't pals, Billy's no so daft as to have pals who'd do that kind of thing – and the story, the story they're giving out, the nasty bits, that's no the way it was. Billy says it's no and he should know. He was there. He was. There. When it happened. He stayed, even if he did nothing he stayed and watched, didn't he, looked on while they hacked up that poor bloke. Poor fucking poof, Joe says. And, ay but ye cannae help thinking, why did he take that road home? Must have been up on the hill. Maybe he tried something on with the lads, maybe made some kind of suggestion. Young lads are touchy about their manhood, maybe he said something, the victim, said the wrong thing and things went wrong from there on, maybe he was asking for trouble. But he died. The poor sod died.

Bet's monologue continues, after the reporters and the police and the social workers have gone, after Joe has given in to a Mogodon slumber, in her head, aloud, all through the sleepless nights. My son, my own bloody son. Up for murder. Near killed me bringing the boy into the world and now he's up for murder. Life over before his sixteenth birthday. A life sentence. One way or another. And if they nail him, how long will he get, how long is life? Bet talks but doesn't get many replies. Joe won't speak about the boy. It's as if he's no longer their son but hers alone, her bairn, her big sullen bairn, her aching burden. Bet cleans her house incessantly, as if she might be able to scrub away the trouble which has wormed its way into every aspect of her life. She can't eat without throwing up. Her stomach has clenched into a burning ball of acid. She can't get a word of sense out of Joe. He's off his work. When he's not making expeditions to the jail, he sits in front of the telly, popping pills. Noreen, who has just started her first year at the big school wakes nightly with the terrors, and wets the bed.

Within a radius of half a mile, four other families are disintegrating in a similar way. Jobs are lost through absenteeism and illness. Friends, not knowing how to be, or unwilling to be drawn into the bloody business, stay away. Sisters and brothers are tormented daily in playgrounds and school corridors. Because of the particular nature of the defence each family is isolated, set against each other. Each new development, reported in the papers or passed on by word of mouth or hearsay, every word – no matter how slight or how unlikely – prompts a chain of adverse reactions in every home.

Down the coast some twenty miles, the once patiently tended garden of a beach cottage is showing signs of neglect. Weeds have choked the flower-beds. Tidal debris has blown up from the sand and been left to settle in the long grass. Inside the cottage a woman sits at her kitchen table, littered with the remains of several meals. Amongst the stale crusts, sour milk, the smears of egg-yolk and jam around which wasps and bluebottles feast without interruption, a square of plastic tablecloth has been cleared. The woman is staring at the square of blue plastic. She has been staring at it all day and the day before that, and seeing on it an ever-changing image of her dead son.

As the wheels of justice roll on laboriously, as men in red silk gowns shuffle papers and pass asides, as they squint through pince-nez at a sheaf of conflicting statements, at forensic reports, evidence and possible alibis, as the fate of five boys is considered in acute and frequently tedious detail, as the jurors inch towards a verdict, the trees turn golden on the street of the three terraces. The dog-walking path and short cut to the London Road remain cordoned off for the time being but the cordons are unnecessary. Nobody other than official visitors – escorted at all times by at least two senior police officers – chooses to push open the squeaking iron gate and walk down three moss-spattered steps to the path which leads to the scene of the crime. The incident is still too fresh in the imagination of even the most sanguine of strollers. Security on the street has been tightened, in spite of the high insurance premium. Locks on gates, extra bolts on doors, electronic alarms. Guard dogs lope and snap behind crackling autumn hedges but still, of an evening, arias by Pavarotti drift through an open window and float above the trees.

# All the Little Loved Ones

I love my kids. My husband too, though sometimes he asks me whether I do; asks the question, Do you still love me? He asks it while I am in the middle of rinsing spinach or loading washing into the machine, or chasing a trail of toys across the kitchen floor. When he asks the question at a time like that it's like he's speaking an ancient, forgotten language. I can remember a few isolated words but can't connect them, can't get the gist, don't know how to answer. Of course I could say, Yes I love you, still love you, of course I still love you. If I didn't still love you I wouldn't be here, would I, wouldn't have hung around just to go through the motions of companionship and sex. Being alone never bothered me. It was something I chose. Before I chose you. But of course that is not accurate. Once you become a parent there is no longer a simple equation.

We have three children. All our own. Blood of our blood, flesh of our flesh etc., delivered into our hands in the usual way, a slithering mess of blood and slime and wonder, another tiny miracle.

*

# Red Tides

In reply to the question my husband doesn't want to hear any of my irritating justifications for sticking around, my caustic logic. He doesn't really want to hear anything at all. The response he wants is a visual and tactile one. He wants me to drop the spinach, the laundry, the toys, sweep my hair out of my eyes, turn round, away from what I'm doing and look at him, look lovingly into his dark, demanding eyes, walk across the kitchen floor – which needs to be swept again – stand over him as he sits at the table fingering a daffodil, still bright in its fluted centre but crisp and brown at the edges, as if it's been singed. My husband wants me to cuddle up close.

Sometimes I can do it, the right thing, what's needed. Other times, when I hear those words it's like I've been turned to marble or ice, to something cold and hard and unyielding. I can't even turn my head away from the sink, far less walk those few steps across the floor. I can't even think about it. And when he asks, What are you thinking? Again I'm stuck. Does it count as thinking to be considering whether there is time to bring down the laundry from the pulley to make room for the next load before I shake off the rinsing water, pat the leaves dry, chop off the stalks and spin the green stuff around the magimix? That's usually what my mind is doing, that is its activity and if it can be called thinking, then that's what I'm doing. Thinking about something not worth relating.

> – What are you thinking?
> – Nothing. I'm not thinking about anything.

Which isn't the same thing. Thinking about nothing means mental activity, a focusing of the mind on the fact or idea of nothing and that's not what I am doing. I've no interest in that kind of activity, no time for it, no time to ponder the true meaning of life, the essential nature of the universe and so on. Such speculation is beyond me. Usually when I'm asked what I'm thinking my mind is simply vacant and so my reply is made with a clear, vacant conscience.

I'm approaching a precipice. Each day I'm drawn nearer to the edge. I look only at the view. I avoid looking at the drop but I know what's there. At least, I can imagine it. I don't want to be asked either question, the conversation must be kept moving, hopping across the surface of our lives like a smooth flat stone.

Thought is not the point. I am feeling it, the flush, the rush of blood, the sensation of, yes, swooning. It comes in waves. Does it show? I'm sure it must show on my face the way pain might, the way pain would show on my husband's face . . .

   – Do you still love me? What are you thinking?

Tonight I couldn't even manage my usual 'Nothing.' It wouldn't come out right. I try it out in my head, practise it, imagine the word as it would come out. It would sound unnatural, false, a strangled, evasive mumble or else a spat denial. Either way it wouldn't pass. It would lead to probing. A strained, suspicious little duet would begin in the midst of preparing the dinner and I know where this edgy, halting tune leads, I know the notes by heart.

(Practice makes perfect. Up and down the same old scales until you can do them without tripping up, twisting fingers or breaking resolutions, without swearing, yelling, failing or resentment at the necessity of repetition. Without scales the fingers are insufficiently developed to be capable of . . . Until you can do it in your sleep, until you *do* do it in your sleep, up and down as fast as dexterity permits. Without practice, life skills also atrophy.)

For years we've shared everything we had to share, which wasn't much at first and now is way too much. In the way of possessions at least. We started simply: one room, a bed we nailed together from pine planks and lasted a decade; a few lingering relics from previous couplings (and still I long to ditch that nasty little bronze figurine made by the woman before me. A troll face, with gouged-out eyes; scary at night, glowering from a corner of the bedroom.) Money was scarce but new love has no need of money. Somewhere to go, to be together is all and we were lucky. We had that. Hell is love with no place to go.

While around us couples were splitting at the seams, we remained intact. In the midst of break-ups and break-outs, we tootled on, sympathetic listeners, providers of impromptu pasta, a pull-out bed for the night, the occasional alibi. We listened to the personal disasters of our friends but wondered, in private, in bed, alone together at the end of another too-late night, what all the fuss was about. Beyond our ken, all that heartbreak, all that angst. What did it have to do with us, our lives, our kids? We had no room for it. Nor, for that matter, a great deal of space for passion.

An example to us all, we've been told. You two are an example to us all. Of course it was meant to be taken with a pinch of salt, a knowing smile, but it was said frequently enough for the phrase to

# All the Little Loved Ones

stick, as if our friends in their cracked, snapped, torn-to-shreds state, our friends who had just said goodbye to someone they loved, or someone they didn't love after all or anymore, as if all of them were suddenly united in a wilderness of unrequited love. While we, in our dusty, cluttered home had achieved something other than an accumulation of consecutive time together.

This is true, of course, and we can be relied upon to provide some display of the example that we are. My husband is likely to take advantage of the opportunity and engage in a bit of public necking. Me, I sling mud, with affection. Either way, between us we manage to steer the chat away from our domestic compatibility, top up our friend's drinks, turn up the volume on the stereo, stir up a bit of jollity until it's time to be left alone together again with our example. Our differences remain.

– Do you still love me? What are you thinking?

Saturday night. The children are asleep. Three little dark heads are thrown back on pillows printed with characters from Lewis Carroll, Disney and Masters of the Universe. Three little mouths blow snores into the intimate bedroom air. Upstairs, the neighbours hammer tacks into a carpet, their dogs romp and bark, their antique plumbing gurgles down the wall but the children sleep on, their sweet breath rising and falling in unison.

We are able to eat in peace, take time to taste the food which my husband has gone to impressive lengths to prepare. The dinner turns out to be an unqualified success: the curry is smooth, spicy, aromatic, the rice dry, each grain distinct, each firm little ellipse brushing against the tongue. The dinner is a joy and a relief. My husband is touchy about his cooking and requires almost as much in the way of reassurance and compliments in this as he does about whether I still love him or not. A bad meal dampens the spirits, is distressing both to the cook and the cooked-for. A bad meal can be passed over, unmentioned but not ignored. The stomach, too, longs for more than simply to be filled. A bad meal can be worse than no meal at all.

But it was an excellent meal and I was wholehearted and voluble in my appreciation. Everything was going well. We drank more wine, turned off the overhead light, lit a candle, fetched the cassette recorder from the kids' room and put on some old favourites: smoochy, lyrical, emotive stuff, tunes we knew so well we didn't have to listen, just let them fill the gaps in our conversation. So far so good.

Saturdays have to be good. It's pretty much all we have. Of us, the two of us just. One night a week, tiptoeing through the hall so as not to disturb the kids, lingering in the kitchen because it's further away from their bedroom than the living-room, we can speak more freely, don't need to keep the talk turned down to a whisper. We drink wine and catch up. It is necessary to catch up, to keep track of each other.

Across the country, while all the little loved ones are asleep, wives and husbands, single parents and surrogates are sitting down together or alone, working out what has to be done. There are always things to be done, to make tomorrow pass smoothly, to make tomorrow work. I look through the glasses and bottles and the shivering candle flame at my husband. The sleeves of his favourite shirt – washed-out blue with pearly buttons, last year's

# All the Little Loved Ones

Christmas present from me – are rolled up. His elbows rest on the table which he recently sanded and polished by hand. It took forever. We camped out in the living-room while coat after coat of asphyxiating varnish was applied. It looks good now, better than before. But was the effort worth the effect?

My husband's fine pale fingers are pushed deep into his hair. I look past him out of the kitchen window, up the dark sloping street at parked cars and sodium lights, lit windows and smoking chimneys, the blinking red eye of a plane crossing a small trough of blue-black sky. My house is where my life happens. In it there is love, work, a roof, a floor, solidity, houseplants, toys, pots and pans, achievements and failures, inspirations and mistakes, recipes and instruction booklets, guarantees and spare parts, plans, dreams, memories. And there was no need, nothing here pushing me. It is nobody's fault.

I go to play-parks a lot, for air, for less mess in the house, and of course because the kids like to get out. Pushing a swing, watching a little one arcing away and rushing back to your hands, it's natural to talk to another parent. It passes the time. You don't get so bored pushing, the child is lulled and amenable. There's no way of reckoning up fault or blame or responsibility, nothing is stable enough, specific enough to be held to account and that's not the point. The swing swung back, I tossed my hair out of my eyes and glanced up at a complete stranger, a father. The father smiled back.

We know each other's names, the names of children and spouses. That's about all. We ask few questions. No need for questions. We meet and push our children on swings and sometimes we stand just close enough for our shoulders to touch, just close enough to feel that fluttering hollowness, like hunger. We visit the park – even in the rain, to watch the wind shaking the trees and tossing cherry blossoms on to the grass, the joggers and dog-walkers lapping the flat green park – to be near each other.

Millions have stood on this very same ledge, in the privacy of their own homes, the unweeded gardens of their minds. Millions have stood on the edge, and tested their balance, their common sense, strength of will, they have reckoned up the cost, in mess and misery, have wondered whether below the netless drop a large tree with spread branches awaits to cushion their fall. So simple, so easy. All I have to do is rock on my heels, rock just a shade too far and we will all fall down. Two husbands, two wives and all the little loved ones.

# Over Her Head

Taking the weight of the trapdoor on the palms of her hands, she lowered it gently. A few inches from the floor, it caught on the torn lino, then thumped into position. Did anybody hear? How loud would the thump have sounded if your ear wasn't right up against the trapdoor? She stayed hunched on the steps, listening for activity in the house until she got a crick in her neck, then clambered down the last few steps and straightened up. The ceiling was low. She had to mind her head on the beams. The household slept on.

What a tip. A right old glory-hole. The bare bulb dangling over the sink did nothing to brighten up the cellar, nor the bundles and boxes stacked in every corner. When you did the washing you never noticed, didn't hang about, you were just up and down with the basket of wet or dry and that was it.

Windowless. The only daylight poked through four finger-sized ventilation holes drilled in the door which led to the back green. Her daughter's wee one had a book with holes just like that. You stuck your fingers through the holes and wiggled them, pretending they were snakes or tigers' tongues or parrots' toes. She put an eye to one of the holes in the door and looked through. She saw the blind man from over the back tap-tapping up the road, a shopping bag swinging from his arm. Always out and about that man, making wee trips to the shops all day long, message-boy maybe for other, less mobile folk in the sheltered housing.

She'd never liked cellars – too cold and dank and close to the dead. During the blitz, she'd shivered under a blanket with her brothers and sisters. Are we in hell? she'd asked. Not yet, her mother had hissed into her ear, but if you don't shush we soon will be. Other people had black-out parties but her mother believed the bombers, like God, could hear your very thoughts and heaped wrath on your head for not taking them seriously.

The house had been heavy with sleep and smelling of children as she let herself out into the sharp morning air. Without warning – as usual – her daughter's family had landed on her the day before. She was happy to have them, but God, did they make a mess. And because of the all-day session it looked like mess was mostly what she'd see of them.

Hoofing it across the park might have helped clear the head, sort out how to cope with what was bound to be thrown at her by the group. You signed yourself up for something and as soon as you'd made the commitment, began asking yourself what was the bloody point. An entire Saturday spent punching pillows and poking holes into other people's private feelings – or ones she felt were better left private – when she could have been getting on with something useful. There was never any shortage of things needing doing.

The cold had made her legs hurt – fiery twinges in the veins – and the hairy winter coat added to her bulk and made her feel like nothing but a fat old woman. It wasn't what you were supposed to feel and she wasn't old, not really. In her mind she felt much the same as when she was a girl but her body betrayed her and everything around her – her grown-up daughter with rampaging toddlers in tow, the yellowed kitchen formica, the growing clutter of medications in the bathroom cabinet – hammered it home that she was getting on. Maybe too far on, too far down the road, to change.

She'd have been better off at the History Group, or the Weight-Watchers, she'd told Gerald. If she'd got the weight down a bit, there's no doubt she'd have felt better. The Weight-Watchers was straightforward, not easy but if you stuck to a plan you got results, results you and everybody else could see. People would stop you in the street, tell you how well you looked. Some might be snidey about it, come right out and say how bloody awful you looked before. But that was just pure spite talking and not worth bothering about.

She could still have gone, unlocked the cellar door – which led into the back green – opened the gate, arrived just a bit late. But once she was under the floor, in her own cellar, she just didn't feel like shifting. Nobody knew where she was. For once she needn't confront anybody and that was what she was so sick of: confrontation. With the family or the group, it was no different. You couldn't have a talk, just a plain old conversation, it was always sparring, one way or another. And if you watched the television, whether it was the news, a nature programme or a drama, what did it all boil down to but confrontation?

She could still go, but why bother? It was all so vague, so airy-fairy, a guessing game with no right answers. She'd tried – sat through session after embarrassing session of painful silences, tears, of insults flying across the room like darts. In the beginning it seemed that maybe something might come of it all. And trying to work out what a person really wanted to say – while they were rabbiting on about something else – was interesting in a way. You learned to read the body language. It didn't take long to figure out that when Jocelyn's smile was stretched across her thin, peaky face, she was really miserable. And when Colin's left foot began to tap he was building up to an outburst. Right at the first meeting somebody had picked on her for keeping her coat on and hugging herself. If she'd been nearer the door that day, she'd have bolted.

She stuck her hand into the poly bag and pulled out a Mars Bar, a tube of Rolos and a packet of Maltesers. She started on the Maltesers, rolling them around her tongue until she'd licked off the chocolate coating. When she finished the packet, she opened the tube of Rolos and chewed her way through them. She'd gone into the newsagent's to buy a paper and come out loaded up with sweets, crisps and juice – enough to stock a children's party. And magazines – a stack of them – some she'd never bought before, only glanced at in the doctor's waiting-room and then always back numbers, the pages cracked and thumbed, greasy from the sweaty palms of sick people.

She wanted to feel better, not worse. It would have been useless talking to Gerald about dropping out. She'd paid the money, the course wasn't cheap, there were no refunds and anyway dropping out was one of her problems. She'd always been in favour of giving something a try but not so much in seeing it through. That was Gerald's department. Slow to shift himself but, when he took something up, he clung to its regularity, its rules and timetables. Nothing bar severe illness prevented him from clipping his moustache, splashing his throat with cologne and brushing up his good jacket. But no bloody wonder. Gerald's nights out were at the old-time dancing and the snooker. She didn't mind the snooker. If he'd had a good game he'd come back merry and conk out. The dancing was another story. Still, as long as he came home at night . . .

Once she'd gone along to the dancing with him, once only. Even bought a dress for the occasion but the peony pink and draped folds hadn't made much difference, hadn't made her feel any better about herself. Gerald loved dancing. Tall, lean, well-turned-out Gerald. She'd enjoyed it herself once upon a time. But to get up on that brightly-lit floor, in full view of everyone, bobbing about like a blimp among that bunch of trim little widows – no way. The whole night she'd sat at the buffet table, bored, irritable, uncomfortable, stuffing chipolatas and chunks of cheddar into her face while Gerald took his pick of partners.

The blankets smelled a bit fusty but they'd been put away clean, and once the old convector got going with its dusty, twangy puffs of warm air and she'd found some plastic sheeting, once she'd spread it out near the heater and laid the blankets and quilt on top, draped the bare bulb with a pink dishtowel to soften the light, once she'd made a wee den for herself in amongst the jumble, the place didn't seem bad at all.

By now she'd have been walking up the tiled path to Jocelyn's black door with the brass knocker, wiping her feet on the 'Come in Peace or Leave me Alone' mat. Then on through the long, sanded hall, following Jocelyn's delicate tread with her clatter, edging on to one of Jocelyn's trendy chairs made of plastic strips which cut into her bum and made her feel fatter than ever. One of these days the stupid chair would snap under her. Made for looking at, not for sitting on, unless you were young and light and not staying long. She'd have been walking into a roomful of people who didn't seem to like each other a bit, yet kept on meeting and making speeches about how they were coming to terms with hating their mother, father, employer, spouse and how good it was to get all that hate out in the open. She didn't hate anyone, unless it was herself and that wasn't the idea at all.

She kicked off her shoes and eased herself under the quilt, a perfectly good old eiderdown with a flowery pattern. She'd hung on to it for years, sure that somebody in the family would find a use for it but she'd had no takers. The pattern was wrong, old-fashioned or something, though why somebody couldn't just cover it with cloth of their choice she didn't know. She swigged some lemonade from the bottle and opened up a magazine and felt like a lady of leisure. Swap the lemonade for champagne, the sweeties for caviare – though the thought of fish eggs turned her stomach – and where was the difference. She had everything she needed: food, drink, heat, plenty to read. Even a potty, left by her daughter on her last visit.

# Over Her Head

*

She could tell from the solid black circles inside the ventilation holes that it was already dark outside. Over her head, she could hear the children doing their after-bath streak round the house. First the quick light feet of the children and then the lumbering tread of the parents trying to catch up with them. Chasing after children was something parents did all their lives, trying to catch them, keep them safe. Another pointless exercise. She blinked and pressed her temples. She was groggy from having dozed throughout the day. She'd drifted in and out of sleep, been dragged out of dreams by sudden eruptions of noise overhead: laughter, songs, rows. The dreams were vivid but hazy too, figures moving through shifting fog, hiding.

That was something else people did all their lives: hide. Inside or out, curtained-off or in full view, they hid their thoughts, feelings, themselves. Did it matter? At the meeting Jocelyn would be scraping away at somebody's surface, poking under somebody's skin, worming into somebody's hidden bits in the hope of digging up something important. But did it matter, any of it? Did it help to remember a time somebody made you feel totally rotten? Wasn't this just dwelling on misery and God knows enough misery threw itself at you without having to dredge up more.

It had done her good, hiding, though she had a touch of bellyache from all the sweeties she'd eaten and was none too pleased by some of what she'd heard said over her head. Who was her daughter calling scared? And of herself? Her daughter was an eejit. They were all eejits and so was she. It was Gerald's night at the dancing, he'd be needing a shirt pressed, she'd promised to babysit so her daughter could meet up with friends. It was always the same. Soon she was going to have to go up for a confrontation.

# The MaMa Chorus

She was someone you noticed, that woman who'd stroll down the dusty Wandsworth Road as if she were at Kew or somewhere, swinging her big hips, turning her fine high head from side to side and giving anybody who happened to be around a wide smile, the kind of smile you'd maybe turn away from, if you had troubles, if you didn't feel up to all that happiness frothing out of her.

Always a deep, winey red, her lipstick, like the vino me and poor old Mum had last year on the Algarve. Shoes strappy, shiny, high, always heels. But she never tottered or hobbled along like some at the day's end, as if all they want is to kick the damn things off as soon as they're home. Carried herself well, Mum would have said. Funny idea, that, like you're two people, one invisible, ferrying the visible one about the place. Funny the way these sayings of Mum's keep popping into my head now she's not around.

Flash gear and heaps of jewellery, fake stuff mostly and the clothes cheap rubbish but that woman had a flair for mix'n'match. Made me feel dull and dowdy, she did, in my navy labcoat and flat pumps. Always dressed up, even if she was only coming down to the shop for toothpaste or mouthwash or a box of throat lozenges. You just had to look at her to know she was her own person.

Must have been our best customer for throat remedies. Spent ages making up her mind. A connoisseur of pastilles, lozenges, gumdrops. Must have sampled every brand we carried. There I'd be, standing at the counter, wondering whether to stock up the Scholl carousel or the depilatories and in she'd stroll. Not much of a talker, but just by being there she livened up the place. I'm not chatty myself – which must have been why Jeremy took me on, him being Mr Noncommunicado personified – and I don't like to pry, especially not when people are coming in for . . . personal things. But throats aren't embarrassing like some parts of the body, so one day I said:
    – You should see about that throat.
    – I can't afford to lose my voice, she said.

Must have been the first time she'd said anything except, 'I'll take the Tunes or Meloids or Strepsils,' the first time I'd really noticed her voice. Deep but clear. As a bell, as Mum would've said. Said she was a singer.
    – That's interesting, I said, So what kind of singing d'you do then? From her big build I was thinking maybe opera.
    – Anything with a contract, she said. Soul to salsa. Mostly studio work. Backing vocals and chorus lines. Ooh Aahs, Dee Dahs and Ma Mas.
No trace of spite or envy creeping in when she added that nobody'd know her name, or be able to put a name to the voice, that she was no big star and too old to become one.

He was gorgeous and knew it, even when he was scowling – dark eyes and a mouth that . . . Young enough to be her son. Didn't seem to bother her but he didn't look over the moon about the googling and squeaky kisses on the nose. He annoyed me. I wanted to run out on to the street and say, 'What's up with your face? Think yourself lucky you've got such a pretty one.' I mean, it's easier, isn't it, if you've got looks on your side. But I don't do that kind of thing so I put the cardboard sun back on its block in the window display and spied on them instead. She managed to get a stiff little smile out of him before they came in.

She bought Fishermen's Friend cough drops for herself and cologne for him, one of the dear ones we keep behind the counter. It would walk off the open shelves. Not as fast as some of the drugs through the back, though. Once he'd been bought a present, Pretty Lips brightened up a bit and began trying on some sunglasses.
– What do you think? he said, turning towards the light.
– Maybe next week, she said and cuddled him out of the shop. Must have spoiled him rotten.

Funny how some little thing can spark you off. I'd never really been one for the music. Mum used to get migraines, so a lot of noise about the house was out of the question. And I was a bit of a shrinking violet when it came to discos. A couple of times I tagged along with a crowd from school, but that was it really. My skin was a mess then, and every time I caught sight of myself – always far too many mirrors at discos – I just wanted to get off home.

Until that woman let me know salsa was something you could sing, I thought it was just some kind of ketchup. I could swear it's what they gave us with our chips on the Algarve. Anyway, at the start of the summer I began taking my radio to work. I knew

Jeremy wouldn't mind if I kept the volume down. Mostly he stays through the back, out of sight. Useless at dealing with the public; even handing over a prescription is an ordeal for Jeremy and God help him if he has to answer a customer query.

The radio was good, filled in the time. And the silence. Jeremy really is very quiet. Apart from his feet and his nose. He's a shuffler. His feet – which are long and thin like the rest of him – never seem to leave the floor. And when he hears something that interests him, he sniffs, like the only way he can take in the information is through his nose. Still, could be worse, as bosses go. At least he leaves me to get on with the job.

As well as the radio I caught a few chart shows on the box. I liked following the bands, seeing who was Number One and how long they lasted, who was the biggest climber of the week, that sort of thing. Music has a shelf-life like anything else but there's something about summer, the lazy way people get in the heat, maybe, which keeps a song buzzing about the place longer than when it's cold. Maybe the heat puts people in the mood for music.

The song which hung on at the top of the charts for most of the summer was a disco number, nothing special really, the usual pump and grind, the kind of thing that just keeps on going like it's on a loop and the only way to end it is fade out or cut. It was the chorus that cracked it. Catchy. Nothing in the way of lyrics, just a few bars when this slinky young thing with a mop of dreadlocks sang solo. I'd find myself humming along though the sound twisted me up inside, like a fire siren or a kid crying. Ma Ma mamama Ma Ma.

*

# The MaMa Chorus

For small premises we carry a decent selection of sunglasses but that woman didn't bring back Pretty Lips for a pair. I don't think she ever brought him back after that. I couldn't say exactly but it must have been around then, late summer, when we were slashing prices on Piz Buin and Ambre Solaire, stocking up on Lemsips and vapour rubs, when things must have fizzled out between them.

You could see she wasn't herself. You'd think she'd got dressed with her eyes shut. Still a smile on her face but a faded one, like most of the tans around town. I wanted to be nice.

– Take your time. No rush, I said.

True. Since Superdrug opened along the road, business had really dropped off. Jeremy was always pestering me to try something fancy with the window display. He was becoming a bit of a pest altogether.

– Have you tried these? I said and pointed out a new throat preparation. Supposed to be very good. On special offer too, I added but the woman just wasn't interested.

The switch to general analgesics got me wondering. She was asking for stuff I couldn't give her without a prescription and, for once, I was sorry I couldn't oblige. I don't hold with folk doping themselves up for every little thing but she was in a bad way. A shadow of her former self, as Mum would have said. That boy must have been a horror. All the same, the pretty ones, think they can get away with murder.

I wanted to cheer her up.

– It must be great to be a singer, I said. To have a gift which nobody can take away.

She looked up at me with big, sad eyes, then began raking through the handypacks on the counter, the Rennies and condoms and razorblades, churning up the stuff. Her nail varnish was chipped.

– They can, she said. And they have.

She'd totally ruined the counter display. I hadn't a clue what she was on about and didn't think I wanted to know, not right then anyway. I certainly didn't want any trouble. We've had trouble in the past and Jeremy panicked and made everything worse. I just wanted her out so I could get the shop sorted. All that small stuff takes ages to put back in place. Didn't want to ask her to leave but I was relieved to see her go. On her way out, she made even more mess, knocking stuff off the aisle shelves, leaving a trail of tubes and bottles rattling about the floor. Luckily nothing broke. Jeremy must have been listening through the back because as soon as the door pinged, he shuffled out to the counter. Funny, he didn't fuss about the mess. Even gave me a hand to tidy up.

– We've seen the last of that one, he said.

Since Mum popped off I've been a free agent, as she'd have put it, which would have been all very well except for Jeremy inviting himself over once a week. The first time he came I was glad of the company but, to be frank, the TV is more company than he is. I don't quite know how to put an end to his visits without causing a problem at work.

Late one night we were sitting in the living-room, Jeremy on the sofa, me in Mum's old armchair. We were having Irish coffees – Jeremy brought the whisky – and watching the box, when who should we see on the screen but that singer woman, weeping big, dramatic tears and telling the viewers that she'd been robbed, that the band who hit the big time last summer had stolen her voice.

# The MaMa Chorus

– Sampled, said the woman. My soul's been sampled.
She bubbled into the camera. Her voice sounded slurry. She was definitely on something, dope or booze, who knows. It was embarrassing. You'd think, with all the other clever things they can do, they could stop showing people breaking down in front of the cameras.

Her head was nodding woozily – like one of those toy dogs folk used to put in the backs of their cars – before they cut to give us a clip of the band singing the hit single. Seeing the video again, you could see that the voice didn't fit the singer. Of course the one with the dreadlocks was miming – everybody does – but it wasn't her own voice she was miming, it was the big woman's voice. The MaMa chorus.

When the camera went back to her, she was sticking another cigarette into her mouth and mumbling on again about her voice being stolen. She sounded rough, hoarse. Jeremy leaned across the sofa. His long, thin arm drooped over my chair and rested on my leg. He sniffed, pressed his skinny fingers into my kneebone and said:

– She could really do with something for that throat.

# Gynae

The face was too big, as if the head had been rolled flat. Blurred; the eyes and mouth just dark smudges. And too close, almost touching her own. All she could see. Her hands went out to push the face away but as she reached out, it backed off, ballooning up into the darkness.

– Just checking.

Night staff. In dark blue. The ones in white took temperatures, blood pressures, urine samples and sat on your bed with a clipboard and a list of questions. The ones in yellow brought clean sheets and tea, if you didn't have NIL BY MOUTH above your bed. Pale green for the theatre crew, plus masks and non-slip clogs. One of them held your hand, the others horsed around, while they knocked you out. They did their business while you were off in limbo land. The jolly butchers. What did the bluecoats do?

– All right?

There was a smell – not a bad smell – familiar, but she couldn't put a name to it. A free-floating memory. No connection, no link to a particular person, place, time. She rubbed her cheek against the pillow, trying to identify the smell. The night nurse must have taken her movement to be a nod because she moved off, a smile spreading like a stain across the lower part of her face. The soles of her shoes made a sucking noise as they detached themselves from the lino.

Calomine? Calendula? Something medicinal but gentle, a balm, not at all like the harsh hospital smells. Camphor, camomile, she had the feeling it was something beginning with Ca. Ca Ca Ca Ca . . . If she could name the smell, she'd be nearer to pinning it down but she went blank after camomile and that wasn't it. Whatever it was, it was comforting and she was in need of comfort. She wasn't all right but neither was anybody else in the ward and she wouldn't be as bad as some. The nurse was out of earshot. She'd have to raise her voice to be heard, which was bound to disturb other patients.

Was there a bell to press? On the wall behind her bed were a couple of unmarked buttons but nobody'd told her what they were for. After they'd taken her particulars – and asked her for the n'th time if she was sure she wanted to go ahead with it – they'd just left her there to wait for her turn to be wheeled along to theatre. Her mouth opened and made the shape of *nurse* but not even a whisper came out. Across the aisle, a woman howled. It was the bleak, naked cry of someone trapped in a bad dream.

She'd been sleeping, dreaming maybe, she couldn't remember, but it had been deep and soothing, the kind of sleep people talked about in books but didn't, in her experience, happen so often. A total escape from awareness. She owed it to the little sturdy nurse – bobbed hair, specs, the trace of an Irish accent – and her needle.

# Gynae

She remembered the chill of meths on her skin, the steel point pushed firmly into her backside, a brief swelling as the morphine sank in, the seductive rush of numbing warmth.

How long had she slept? How many hours had passed? That was what mattered, passing the hours, days, God help them weeks, staring at the telly or the ceiling, using up the time in baths, meals, medication, sleep. In Gynae people didn't talk much and didn't ask what you were in for. Too touchy an area: terminations and blocked tubes, women getting rid of babies, women desperate to conceive. If they could have done a swap . . .

Her back-to-front gown felt damp. She slid her hand over the sheet. Damp also. Maybe just sweat. Maybe that was all it was but she'd have to look, to check because the nurse hadn't. The light switch was in an awkward place, high on the wall behind the bed. She had to turn over onto her side and hoist herself up, supported by an arm which felt as if the bones had dissolved, as if it hadn't been used for a very long time. The stitches tugged as she lunged for the light. God Almighty. Worse than before. A flood.

She sat up in bed, holding the sodden red sheet away from her matching gown, staring at the strange brightness of the blood. How could it be her own, all that from a small incision at the navel? She looked like one of the battle victims she'd seen on the lunchtime news, when there was no lunch because they hadn't done her yet, hadn't opened her up. To get away from the tormenting smell of food which wafted into the ward from the corridor, she'd moved through to the patients' sitting-room. Nothing like NIL BY MOUTH above your bed to whet the appetite.

An auxiliary had been dusting the seats.

– Glad I don't work *there* she'd said, as footage from yet another war-torn city was blasted across the screen. Bombs and bloody corpses. Hospitals bursting at the seams.

# Red Tides

– What a world, eh? The things people do to each other. Never watch the news. Gets me down, so it does. *Hello!* magazine, that's my cup of tea. Everybody's happy, that's what I like to see. Gives you a wee lift. Want a loan of this week's issue?

She'd said no to *Hello!*

Like a moth, the night nurse fluttered towards the light and drew the curtains round her bed. More red. Red and pink stripes to stare at while the nurse went off without a word, to find something or someone. At the far end of the ward a cistern hissed. Did she need to pee? The last time they'd made her use a commode. The swaying curtains were making her nauseous.

She shouldn't still be here, wouldn't have been if things had gone to plan. She'd told the nurse, the sturdy one with the needle, she'd told her she had to get home, the kids would be upset, she'd promised them a bedtime story. And anyway she couldn't waste any more time on all this, she'd have to be back on her feet the next day, or the day after at the outside, have to be fit for work. If she took the injection she couldn't go home . . .

– One thing at a time, Christine, said the nurse, the only one out of everybody she'd seen who called her by her first name. It had seemed more caring somehow and she had been in a state, the pain severe, and the morphine had taken it away, taken everything away for a while. Even now she still felt detached from her body, distant, except for the wound. All she felt in touch with was the wound, invisible under a sodden dressing, only the incision at the navel linked her with her body.

A low rumble of trolley wheels. The curtains parting like the Red Sea. Another face. Yellow coat. Armful of starched linen.

– What a state you're in, said the auxiliary, sighing at the sight of it, her, and she felt embarrassed by the mess, the trouble, about having to sit on a chair while a stranger changed her bed, covered the sodden dressing with a fresh lint pad – We'll leave that to the doctor – and dressed her in a clean gown. Like a baby, a bloody baby. She'd gone through a load of linen, made extra work for everybody.

Something had been taken away. That had been the point of the hospital visit, to take something, no, the *possibility* of something away from the invisible regions of her body. That had been done. She had been done. Doctored. She'd volunteered. The decision had been made under no pressure from anyone and it had seemed like a good idea, a practical one at any rate, one which would simplify the future, make it manageable. But something else had been taken away.

A white-coated nurse breezed through the curtains, followed by a young male doctor, in theatre green. He held out his hand to her but before she realised that she was meant to shake it, the hand had been retracted. She could feel a wild giggle bubbling up from the pit of her stomach, trying to free itself, to erupt into the sleeping ward. She mustn't laugh. It would hurt to laugh and anyway, it wasn't funny, there was nothing at all to laugh at.

But God, he was so young to be left in charge. Just a boy, white-faced under the light, unruly red curls falling into his eyes. Not exactly Doctor Kildare. As a kid she'd watched the debonair Chamberlain on telly and – along with thousands or maybe millions of other female viewers – fantasised about being laid up with some critical (but not disfiguring) injury and coaxed back to health by a concerned and attentive Kildare.

A lot of bloody nonsense. Nobody in their right mind would want to meet a man they fancied under these conditions. A woman, even a very young woman, would have been better. A woman would have made more sense. Why were there so many men in Gynae? How could a man decide what best to do with bits he didn't have? And what in God's name attracted them to specialise in that department? Were they all perverts or what?

The smell was still there. Maybe it was in the linen. Knowing what it was wasn't going to help any but it was something to think about, something else. Maybe it was in the air. The flowers? Plenty flowers about the place, though none at her own bedside. She'd had no visitors. No need, she'd be in and out the same day, that was the plan. But the plan had fallen through and when they decided – the smarmy young surgeon who cracked jokes about bimbos and bikini lines and the nice nurse with the needle – when they decided to keep her in overnight, she'd wished to God that one of those fit people who filled up the ward after the evening meal with chat and chocolates, was there to visit *her*. But no flowers. Elsewhere she liked them; in the wild, in a garden, a vase on the kitchen table. But not in hospital. There was something stiff and lifeless about the florist's sprays, the functional bunches of cheery daisies, tight, fleshy rosebuds and papery carnations. Carnations. Could it be the carnations?

She felt stupid being wheeled through the ward flat on her back, tried to sit up, was gently but firmly restrained by the nurse, put in her place, in the hands of two tired-looking kids . . .

Notices in the corridor. NO SMOKING. GIVE UP SMOKING. PATIENTS' CHARTER. What did that say? She'd read it through that morning as she waited to be admitted, waited to hand over her body . . . courteous . . . prompt . . . ensure. What was it that they would ensure? What was it that she had a right to expect?

# Gynae

The overhead light in the theatre was weak and ineffectual, sick-looking. Gone the bright daytime buzz of the operating-room, gone the loud, hairy porter who showed off his tattoos, leered at the *ladies* and jollied them along to the chopping block. At night the room was grey and dreary and deserted.

She was rolled off the trolley on to the table, a surprisingly narrow metal and rubber affair, and left on her own again. It was the way of it. Entrances and exits. And then the voices off – whispers, laughter, the well world going on as usual on the other side of the curtain. Had they gone for a bloody tea-break?

She could do with a drink. Nothing all day. NIL BY MOUTH. A drink would make her feel better. And a bite to eat. Bread and water would do fine. If she could get hold of the one who'd changed her bed . . . Why hadn't she thought to ask at the time? She was the one to ask. Tea was one of her duties. No point in asking the wrong person, the doctor, say. Doctors didn't deal with tea.

There was something worrying about the way the two of them were passing intruments back and forward, and all that rattling and clinking. It seemed . . . experimental, like kids making up a game, a kind of medical Mad Hatter's Tea Party. The nurse couldn't find the bloody scissors. The doctor was holding a length of catgut which looked like a guitar string. He was squinting at the stuff with the curiosity people show for something they've never seen before. She felt horribly alert. She'd seen more than enough and they hadn't even started yet. If they'd just give her a bloody general like the first time, instead of a local, all she'd know would be a fizzing tingle in the veins, then blackout.

But it was the nurse who blacked out, just after the doctor peeled off the dressing. He held it out to the nurse for her to dispose of but she shook her head. Her eyelids flickered rapidly. Her face turned the colour of the walls. She stepped clear of the operating table and flopped on to the floor. The doctor gawped at the body on the floor and the body on the table, stupefied by panic. The desire to run away was written all over him, yet he did nothing except stare at his hands as if he were counting them and wondering, Why so few?

Beneath her dressing the blood had pooled thick and dark and in an alarming quantity. As the doctor dithered between cleaning up the patient and resuscitating the nurse, she lay on the table and looked up at the ceiling. Again, a giggle – or was it a scream – bubbled up from her guts.

– Can I do anything to help? she said. Help was needed and at that moment she was the only person available to supply it.

# Hormones

According to my sums I shouldn't go out. Going out costs money
and what I'll take in my purse is already spoken for, earmarked.
Besides, my husband is still not speaking to me after this morning.
His face is a picture of long-sufferance and resentment. The wee one
is being clingy and whingey. The big one is jealous because the wee
one is getting what attention there is, which isn't much. I can't give
much tonight. Not what is wanted anyway. The big one is muscling
in on the cuddles and nipping the wee one on the sly. A noisy and
tearful scene is more than likely. Added hassle for my husband. More
reason to resent me but, no matter what, I'm going out. Into the
night. On my own. Again.

It's like turning a corner and coming face-to-face with a crazed
dog. By now I should know ahead of time what to expect and lie
low, keep my head down until the slavering beast has dragged
itself off into a dark corner and licked itself to sleep. Having it
happen on such a regular basis I should have developed an early-
warning system, some good old female intuition, something. But
nothing. Until it's too late, the damage done, there's no telling
why I feel like murdering every man I meet or screwing him silly.

# Red Tides

*

Out or in it's the same. In shops, on the street, the bus, in the park, on the telly, inside my head, I see men. I stare at men. Constantly. Indiscriminately. The prematurely white-haired man who comes to fix the stereo, the pretty Moroccan boy in the sandwich-bar with oiled curls and chiselled cheekbones, the sandy-haired stone-mason sipping tea on the wall outside my gate . . . I could go on for ever. I look at them all, with intent. It's as if someone has flicked a switch, as if my blood has changed direction, is flowing the wrong way. I feel flushed, chilled. The blood rushes, then ebbs. Do I crackle and spark, sizzle, glow, hum like I'm about to blow a fuse? No, but it feels like I do.

Normally I don't notice men much and they don't notice me, apart from my husband and the department which makes more than enough men to be going on with. At work I try to look neutral. I wear dark colours. I like the tidiness, the simplicity of black, navy, charcoal, and I suit them. Strong colours make me look anaemic, which I may well be. Yet I feel too full of blood. I avoid wearing anything remotely sexy. There's enough to deal with in a working day without that lot getting ideas. Weekends and holidays, out with the kids, I wear what I like and it doesn't matter a damn. I'm invisible to men. I could be walking down the street in my birthday suit and wouldn't even raise a whistle from builders, road-diggers, bin-men, leaf-sweepers, shopkeepers or bench-loafers. Who needs purdah when you've got kids in tow?

Normally it's women I notice, watch. Not with any dubious intentions, simply because I am one. It's normal and healthy to make connections and comparisons. I'm not saying that a woman has never made me think of murder or sex but that's a bit more out of the ordinary. At the moment I'm trying to pin down the normal, usual, habitual me, to put it under glass and examine it. It's well past time.

My memory is selective. So are other people's, if friends, family, and bump-into acquaintances are anything to go by. We dredge up the same junk over and over. My memory is full of holes. Things slip through it, like a net. I let them go. Forget what I don't want to remember. Remember what I don't want to forget – though what's remembered and what's forgotten rarely bear much relation to what I started with. Times change. Time changes. Trite, but true. I've fished out some little snippet, hauled it out of the sludge, held it up to the light for one last look and found that time, or neglect, had scoured it smooth, shone it up in a way which made other, more cherished memories seem dull and trivial.

An example? Later, maybe.

My memory is no help because it is no good at dates. History was a subject at school which I dropped as soon as I could. Because of dates, partly. And partly because the history teacher also taught R.E. in her free periods. She had a round, shy, pasty face which reddened at all the awkward words in the Bible, like begat and virgin and circumcision. I liked those words, liked how they sounded and wanted – but wasn't given – an explanation. Also I wanted to see the deep blush redden Miss Macdonald's pasty face from the slippy, colourless collar of her blouse to her wispy halo of colourless hair.

Bear with a sore head. Screaming hyena. Crabbit bitch. I've been called all of these already today, the day isn't over yet, and the night stretches before me, paved with good intentions like the road to hell, ruin, or sin, I can't remember which. *Tartar* is what my granny would have called me, did call me when I was wee and enraged. I didn't mind. It was a good name, especially the way she said it, rolling the Rs round her mouth like the aniseed balls and zebra-striped boilings she loved to suck and crunch. Ach, ye're a wee Tartar, so ye are. It made me think of the dreamy windswept horseback rider in billowing pantaloons who starred in a TV ad of the time. Turkish Delight. Full of Eastern Promise. I wanted to be both the masterful raider with scimitar eyes and his languid, bejewelled beauty with honeyed lips, waiting for him on a sparkling sand dune.

That was it, the example, the memory. It just bubbled up to the surface without any effort. A TV ad. My granny's taste in sweeties. Androgenous fantasies. Dear, dear. Of course Tartars probably spent much more time chopping off heads than popping sweatmeats into the mouths of ladyfriends but I wasn't to know, was I? As far as I was concerned, being called a Tartar was far too romantic and exotic to be taken as real trouble.

Normally I am quiet and easy-going but today things have tipped into the fraught zone. My daughter got it. My husband got it. The department got it. My tongue. The stuff that rolled off my tongue – pure poison. Horrible. The child stuck her fingers down her throat, made a face like sick and hid in the Wendy House. The father attempted to intervene, to reconcile mother and daughter. All the thanks he got was a mouthful of foulness from me and a kick in the shin from her. By the time I had my coat on and we'd reached a state of smouldering silence, which was as far as any of us – being competitively stubborn – was prepared to go towards a truce, I was already late for work.

Though I can't forward-plan on my own behalf, can't prepare for my hellish mood swings, I like to be punctual. No, it's not that I actually feel pleased by getting in on time, I just hate to be late. I try to give myself more than enough time to get up and out. If I have to hurry I get rattled and handless. By the time I reached work today I was a seething mess of guilt and rage and rush, someone to steer clear of.

To get anything out of a diary, I'd have to remember to check my dates several times a day. I have one, a large, hardbacked desk diary with the university crest on the cover and a page for each day. But it's public property and no way would I enter anything personal. The desk diary is the departmental bible. As soon as I have hung up my coat, I open it. It makes a soft whirring sound as I leaf through the smooth pages. The paper is good quality, medium-weight, with a faint sheen which makes it easy to handle. They like their classy stationery around here. I spread today on my desk and put on a pot of coffee.

The department would be lost without the desk diary to remind them of future obligations, chores, and damned nuisances in their lives. Treats as well, of course. How would an academic department cope without Staff – Student Liaison sherry parties? Not that there's often any actual sherry. Too dear and the students haven't studied how to sip. Quantity is what the young ones like. Big drinks. The more the merrier and if they throw it all up later who cares? So it's two-litre screwtops or carton plonk I order.

# Red Tides

Though I'm employed to deal with the working life of the department, to make sure that they know where, when and on what subject their lectures are, remember to attend board meetings, file grant applications and so on, there is a good deal of overspill. Most of the staff are inept beyond words at keeping tabs on their lives, which makes me an indispensable ready reference. If I'm off sick, or on holiday, the place goes to pot. They can't even cope with me being late. I hear them shuffling to and fro in the corridor – I know them all by their feet – anxiously waiting for their fix of coffee and chitchat. Why nobody can take it upon himself to put on the bloody coffee once in a while I don't know, but that lot would rather loiter in the corridor with their tongues hanging out. Who says it's nice to be needed? Today they can all just piss off. Hole up in their stuffy, book-lined burrows. Get on with what they're paid for instead of cluttering up my office.

What some people need done for them. I remind them to go to the dentist, the bank, to buy presents for their wives – though more often than not it's me who shops for the presents, in my lunch hour. I buy good stuff: silk scarves, rare plants, pretty knicknacks, perfume, things I'd like for myself, treats. Needless to say all I ever get in return is soap or sweets at Christmas. I put some thought into the presents I buy. I bring their wives pleasure.

Mummy, matron and sometimes other things, but that's another story. *Discretion and diplomacy are two of Marilyn's most outstanding features* – so said my reference for the job. You certainly need both in these cloak-and-dagger corridors. *Marilyn's office is a warm, fertile haven of coffee and smalltalk, a revitalising oasis in a desert of archives and intellectual fencing.* So Phil, the professor, is fond of saying. One of his spluttering learned witticisms. God, how he loves to take the long way round. As far as Phil is concerned there's no such thing as a simple sentence. *Arguably* is his favourite word. His dictation is a nightmare. A clever man but a piss-awful human being. They say academics love their work more than their wives and in Phil's case it's true. Nothing makes him perk up more than having me call his wife and tell her he's working late.

Nobody here ever thinks, not properly. Normally I don't mind doing their thinking for them. I enjoy it, I'm good at it. I write their papers. Not the material, the facts – they know their stuff or, if they don't, they know which books to consult. They know how to pile up information. But I'm the one who sorts it out. I give the students something they can use, a hand-out which has full stops and paragraphs, a plan. If I typed up the junk I'm given without making amendments right, left and centre, the poor students would be bamboozled. And who'd take the rap? A girl I know lost her job for not correcting a professor's spelling errors.

Anyway, diaries. No use. First, a diary is work. Second, it reminds me that there's a date beyond which I'll make no more entries. Stuff that kind of reminder. I'm neither young enough nor old enough for morbidity. I don't give it the time of day. Even if I try to put my mind to important things like life and death, it always finds its way back to shopping lists and sums. I add, subtract. I round up figures and shuffle them from one column to another. I underestimate, overestimate. Hope for windfalls. Make allowance for catastrophes. I forward-plan, back-pedal, budget, cut corners. Somebody has to. As far as departmental finances are concerned, it's me who's left holding the baby. The professor's too busy finding a publisher for his latest book to do more than cast a hasty eye over the accounts. I know where every last penny goes, chase people for chits. I'm wise to all the fiddles. I liaise with the Finance Office, salesmen, maintenance engineers, the lot.

Gerry, the repair man, came to my office today, to look at the printer, which has been playing up as usual. Mid-afternoon and everyone who wasn't teaching was safely up two flights of stairs, sprawled on squeaky plastic seats in the seminar room, debating the fate of research grants. Gerry's no bother. Knows his job and gets on with it. I like that in a man. He takes off his jacket, rolls up his sleeves and begins poking away at the printer. He has nice arms. Smooth, freckly. Even though you can't help but get covered with ink, fixing printers, his fingernails are always clean as a surgeon's when he comes in. He smells of something tangy, like limes. Likes to talk, pass on the gossip. Tells a good story. Told me he was going out on the town tonight. Mentioned the venue. Said to drop by if I was stuck for company.

It's a filthy night. Nobody is on the street. The wind is blowing litter over the cobbles and the rain into my face. My hair sticks to my cheeks and wet drips down the back of my neck. I walk quickly, head down, battling against the wind. Just right. As it should be. What I need. I won't take the bus, I'll walk. Don't know where I'm going but I'll find somewhere, a smart café, a smoky pub, a place where there are people. Men. A warm finger of light will beckon, laughter burst through a swing door, a jukebox song stop me in my tracks. I'll find the place. Soon. I don't need to find it yet, not quite yet. Foul weather makes going out a bit of a battle; and my hormones are up for that.

# The Fence

The two big girls looked at each other. They were the same age:
five-and-three-quarters. Both had greenish, slanty eyes, long
fairish hair and a missing front tooth. Both were tousled-looking,
in spite of their mothers' earlier attempts to tidy them up. They
liked each other on sight. The town girl had come dressed for the
country, in T-shirt, leggings and wellies, though it was a warm,
dry day. The country girl was wearing a crumpled party dress but
changed immediately into T-shirt, leggings and wellies, adding a
garish rag of a cardigan, embarrassing her mother.

– Not that dreadful old thing. It's fit for the bucket.

– I think it's a beautiful cardigan, said the town girl. I wish I'd
brought my cardigan. We could have been like twins!
The country girl paraded the shapeless cardigan with pride and,
having gained an ally, a large dose of defiance.

While the town parents were being shown round what was –
even by their own lax standards – a stunningly messy country
house, the country girl took the town girl out to play in the
filthiest ditch in the vicinity. Both girls had to be scrubbed
thoroughly before lunch.

*

– I hate beetroot.

– No you don't. Last time you had it . . . No, please, no. The window doesn't like beetroot.

– Neither do I.

– Does anybody like beetroot? Hands up anyone in this room who likes beetroot and I'll give them a prize.

– So. What are you working on these days?

– What kind of prize?

– I want a prize, I want a prize!

– There's no need to shout. Nobody's deaf, you know.

– Grandad's deaf.

– Yes but Grandad's not here, is he?

– But I know him. You said Nobody's deaf *you know* . . .

– I see your name in the papers from time to time.

– Sorry . . . sorry to interrupt but . . . could you move that . . .

– Never mind. No sense in crying over spilt milk.

– I didn't do that, I didn't! She pushed me.

– Did not. You're a bloody fibber.

– What was that?

– What was what? I didn't hear anything. Did you hear anything?

– Do you do a lot for the papers these days?

– What did you *say*?

– Nothing. You said . . .

– Yes you did, you said *bloody*.

– So? You say bloody. Why shouldn't I?

– Shall I get something to clean up that milk?

– Well I'm kept fairly busy these days. Lucky really, the way things are going.

Lunch was an altogether fraught affair. Nobody really knew each other. The country father and town mother had bumped into each other a few times, years back, had recently bumped into each other again and – for the sake of the children – agreed to meet up. The food was served – no, neither served nor passed around, dumped on the table and up for grabs – in the conservatory, the only bright and clutter-free area in the house. A massive rambling jasmine draped itself across the one wall like a lacy curtain, giving off an overpowering odour of smoky Chinese tea.

The tranquil surroundings were completely lost under the prevailing racket which five young children (four girls, one boy) generated at the table. The town parents were slightly hungover from the night before and the noise set their heads thumping. The country parents had an extra child to deal with, a tired boy who kicked, screamed and lunged at every breakable or spillable object within reach of his cross little fists. The mother pleaded politely with this child and that, the father was politely firm but all their pussyfooting was having no effect, unless it was to spur the children on to even more disgusting acts of mutiny. At the table, the big girls sealed their friendship by behaving as badly as possible. They were banished to the garden immediately after pudding, which was exactly what they wanted. The only person to eat a decent meal was the youngest child, who sat stolidly in her high chair, pushing into her mouth whatever she was given.

The big girls ran ahead up the steep path through the woods, whooping and screeching like old friends, though they'd only known each other an hour. The mothers trailed alongside each other, gazing indulgently at their little ones, who pattered along, picking up leaves and stones, clambered over fallen logs and, as there were no toys to fight over, ignored each other. For conversation, the women compared notes on their children: whose woke the earliest, went to bed latest, was up most often during the night, was out of nappies first; whose was a picky eater, whose had problems with allergies, rashes, bowels. Then they compared notes on their partner's performance as a father: did he cook, wash up, put the kids to bed, get them dressed in the morning; did he clean the toilet? That was usually a reliable topic, something to agree about.

At the foot of the path, the boy, even more wabbit and grizzly than at lunchtime, clung to his tricycle, demanding that his daddy pull him, on his trike, up the hill, not by hand but by means of the shepherd's crook the country father had brought out with him. The town father ignored the other man's futile attempts to persuade the boy to leave the trike where it was and pick it up on the way back. The town father wasn't impressed by the country father's crook, which struck him as ostentatious. It wasn't as if there were any sheep around which needed to be rescued.

The town father lit a cigarette, took a deep drag of country air and looked up at the trees, wondering what they were called. Didn't trees have families, too? He was relieved that lunch was over. At least in the open, the noise had, to an almost tolerable extent, dissipated. As far as he was concerned, he'd done his bit: contributed to the table talk when called upon to do so, supplied the facts and figures when pressed. At that moment he'd have been happy to sit down, under a tree of any kind, and read the newspaper he'd optimistically brought out with him.

The mothers were comparing notes on the relative merits of staying at home with children and going back to work. They hovered around the area of dense woodland where the big girls had last been seen. They hadn't been seen, or heard – which was more significant – for some time and a mild waver of panic crept into the mothers' conversation. The country father, lugging his load, a harried smile drawn tight across his face, caught up with the town father. Over the persistent girning of his son, he began to explain the difficulties, in the country, of *fitting in*. There were, he said, the rich and the poor, who didn't, wouldn't talk to each other. At all. For years on end. And themselves, who sat on the fence, who'd talk to anyone, if they were given the chance. The rich owned land, the poor were farmworkers and redundant miners. The country father sympathised with the miners. But couldn't find any personal good reason not to speak to some of the other side, like Major Cunningham and his good-looking daughter. Married to a musician. A successful musician. Interesting people.

– EEEEYYAAHHH!

The big girls burst out of the bushes, bared their bums, stuck out their tongues and cackled like hyenas in at the kill. The mothers smiled vaguely, relieved that their daughters had not fallen in a ditch, or had their clothes torn to shreds by the rusty barbed wire which snaked through the undergrowth. The town father laughed. The country father threw down his crook and marched over to them and, in spite of his naked rage, said something very quiet and restrained to them, which nobody else could hear. For the time it took to pull up their knickers, the girls were suitably shamefaced. But one look at each other and they resumed their hideous cackling and ran off up the path. None of the adults, now bunched together and inching forwards in the oblique manner of a spider, could be bothered running after them.

– They really seem to be getting on well, don't they?
– Don't they?
– It's amazing how children can just *get on* like that, become friends straight away.

– You'd think they'd known each other for years.

– Of course it's all black and white with children. Clear cut.

– Hmmm, well, I wouldn't say, I mean sometimes it can be a bit more . . . complicated.

– Anyway, they've hit it off, which is just as well.

– It wouldn't have been fun for anybody if that pair hadn't got on.

– It would not.

The path joined another and the two forks merged into a broader single track. From the other path, a fluffy golden retriever bounded towards the junction. Screaming in fright, the town girl made a dash for her mother. A leashed dog in the park was one thing, a free-ranging one another. Not that the animal had any interest in the girl. It stopped at the junction and barked idiotically until its owners, the Cunninghams, appeared: a silver-haired grandmother (peony lips, trench coat and sunglasses – though the sky was overcast), a ruddy grandfather (blazer, walking stick, dog lead and whistle), their tall, big-boned daughter (boots and breeches, wax jacket, silk scarf knotted tightly at the neck) and her two girls (mousy pigtails tied with bows, identical Shirley Temple dresses). The country girl yanked the town girl's hand away from her mother's sleeve and clutched it between her own.

– Lovely day.

– Isn't it.

– Mmmnn, yes. How are you all?

– Oh, just fine, aren't we?

– Jolly good.

– Are you scared of the dog, dear?

– Put it on a lead! Put it on a lead!

# The Fence

– It doesn't chase children, dear. Just birds.

– PLEASE!

The grandmother sighed and smiled.

– James, the dog.

– Jolly good.

The grandfather gave his whistle a couple of blasts and the dog obediently trotted over to be tethered.


– I say, your lot are getting big.

– Aren't they. And yours. My goodness.

– Yes they're growing out of everything. Cost a fortune, little girls, don't they?

– Mmmnnn.

– And you never get it back with girls, do you? No matter what they say about equality and all that, they never really pay their way. Did you know that in some places people just do away with girl babies, flush them down the river.

– I've read about it. China is it? Or India, maybe.

– I say, you two. Come and say hello. Don't be rude now.

– Yes, why don't you two go and say hello to the Cunningham girls? I'm sure they'd like to meet you.

– Well we wouldn't like to meet them.

– Well, I say. That settles that, doesn't it? Horrors, little girls, the lot of them.

– No social graces.

– No. Quite right too. No sense in beating about the bush.

The girls in dresses flounced on ahead, pigtails swinging. The other two took up the rear of the straggling procession. The town parents also lagged a bit, inspecting the greenery with exaggerated interest.

\*

– Well, this is where we leave you.

– Jolly good to see you.

– Yes. Nice to see you too.

– You must come over some time.

– Mmmnn, yes. That would be nice, wouldn't it?

They had stopped in front of a tall house (white walls, sandstone facings, too many windows to count). Major Cunningham pushed open the wrought iron gate and ushered the dog inside. His granddaughters pushed past him and the dog and positioned themselves on the inside of the sturdy fence, directly in front of the girls in T-shirts, mud-streaked leggings and caked wellies.

– This is OUR HOUSE.

– So?

– ALL OUR HOUSE. And OUR FENCE.

– So?

The girl inside the fence spoke with a hissing lisp. Outside, the town girl folded her arms and pounded the ground with her boot, the way bulls do before they charge.

– OUR HOUSE, OUR FENCE AND OUR GARDEN.

It was quite a garden: a long sloping lawn; scalloped borders, sculpted bushes, a stone sundial inlaid with brass, an elaborate rockery tumbling down to an oval pond where a bronze mermaid sat and combed her verdigrised locks.

– You can't come in here.

– We don't want to. So there.

– So there.

But the town girl longed to get in and see the mermaid up close and so did the country girl, to show it off to her friend. Both of them liked mermaids. That was why they were friends: they liked the same things: mermaids, princesses, My Little Ponies and all kinds of stuff their parents said were nonsense.

– If you come in here, we'll . . . KICK YOU!

– OH NO YOU WON'T!

– OH YES WE WILL, WE'LL KICK YOU KICK YOU KICK YOU!

– Girls, girls. Please. Goodness me.

– If you kick us we'll CUT OFF YOUR FEET!

– Well, we'll, we'll . . . SHOOT YOU! Our daddy's got a gun and we know how to work it, so there.

– SHOOT YOU SHOOT YOU SHOOT YOU!

– Come now, that's enough. Into the house you two. Chop chop. Vicious little monsters aren't they? Terribly nice to see you all. Well, goodbye.

– Yes, nice to see you.

– And nice to meet . . . your friends.

– Mmnnn.

– Goodbye.

– Goodbye.


The boy scoots down the hill on his trike, triumphantly. The mothers carry the little ones in their arms. The town father walks with them, carrying the leaves and twigs which have been collected on the walk. The country father, who can't remember where he left his crook, roots around in the bushes. The big girls meander down the hill, arms linked. Looking back at the fence, they promise themselves they'll each have a mermaid one day, but not mottled or mossy, a clean, silky mermaid with a shimmery tail and green eyes like their own and sparkles of water in her hair, like tiny rainbows.

\*

# Red Tides

– Well, those two got on well, didn't they?
– Mmnnn. Aren't children so direct?

# Jumping into Bed with Luis Fortuna

Dear Luis,

You don't know me and I hope you don't mind me writing to you like this. You must have many admirers. I hope you do. You deserve them. But if you really hate people posting their opinions to you, please read no further. I just wanted to say . . .

She scored through what she had written.

She didn't believe in heroes but still, in spare moments downtown, she'd nip into bookshops in search of his latest novel. Recently he'd become easier to track down. A prize-winning film had been made of one of his books and new novels and reprints carried on the cover – along with the title and his name, Luis Fortuna, in bigger print than previously – the flier: Author of *Lair of the Panther Princess*. His titles were always tacky or weird or misleading.

She'd got herself anchored: house, job, man, kids. The backpack was long gone, she was well and truly stuck. To compensate for her lack of mobility she watched travel programmes on TV, learned to cook Indian pastries and Mexican soups, listened to music from Africa and Brazil and attended a night class in Spanish.

Dear Luis,

You don't know me and I hope you don't mind me writing to you out of the blue like this. I contacted your publishers but they wouldn't give me your address. Maybe they thought I was cracked or after money I don't know, but I expect you'll be pleased to know that you are being protected against that kind of postal nuisance. Anyway, they suggested I sent a letter via their London office which would then be forwarded to their New York office and on to the capital city of the country where you are presently living – they would not even tell me that! There, I was told, it would probably be held in a box for twenty-one days, when – if it had not been uplifted – it would be returned to sender or destroyed. So who knows whether this will ever reach you . . .

He was as much a vice as a pleasure. Some mornings, alone in the house, faced with unwashed dishes, unswept floors, unmade beds, the sight of someone else's washing flapping above the back green in a good drying wind which shouldn't be missed, she'd let herself be seduced. Drawing the curtains, kicking off her shoes, she'd jump into bed with Luis Fortuna.

That was what it felt like, not just reading about some made-up characters, no, she was getting to know him personally, intimately. She had seen a couple of snaps on flyleafs. He was dark-haired, clean-shaven. Between his brows a small frown curled like a wormcast. Around his mouth was the hint of a smile, of mischief. That's what had got her hooked in the first place. When she put him aside and made a start on the beds or floors or dishes, it was with a vague thrill of guilt, as if she had not been in bed with a book, but a lover.

She wasn't a great reader, not like her husband John who was a glutton for printed matter, consuming at high speed whatever he picked up. When she read at all she did it slowly, stubbornly, with resistance. Every so often she'd bring home the permitted quota of bulky hardbacks from the library but more often than not they were returned unread. Not that she had chosen rubbish, she was choosy but most of the worthy stuff weighed on her, tired her out.

Luis Fortuna was a serious writer, no doubt about it. He didn't shy away from trouble – the agonies and slight aches, the huge and tiny tragedies. But he was funny. He could make her laugh out loud. And he understood women so well, got under their skin, into their minds, didn't present them as saints or tarts; he was critical, bitchy but there was an affinity, a relish for all their contradictions and subterfuge, their secret longings. Her husband was put off Luis Fortuna by the trashy titles and lurid covers and she was glad. She had him to herself.

She imagined meeting him somewhere; anywhere would have done but she fixed on a terrace café, a sunny open place facing a busy plaza in an invented Rio or Buenos Aires. They'd sit under a spindly tree with small, fine leaves which rustled in the warm breeze, watching other people. He'd be rude but charming. He'd catch the eye of a woman, perhaps a rich, well-dressed woman, purse his Latin lips then turn back to the table, take her hand in his and begin a sad but side-splitting tale of a rich and well-dressed woman.

Dear Luis,

I expect you receive a great deal of fan mail and perhaps you have an aversion to it. If so, please don't waste your time reading further because all I really want to say is that I've been reading your books for years and have found every one . . . a real treat . . . immensely satisfying . . . an astounding feat of imagination . . . compelling . . . dazzling . . . a winner . . . deeply moving . . . absorbing . . . spellbinding . . .

She tried all kinds of stuff she had seen on the back covers, phrases taken from articles and reviews, phrases written by professionals, by people who had been paid for their words and it all sounded inadequate or false. But she had to say something if she was going to write the letter at all, she couldn't write and say she'd read all his books without saying something. Version after version of the letter was scored through, crushed, binned. What she ended up with was:

Dear Luis,

I just wanted to say that I think your books are great. Please write more.

Such a skimpy note didn't seem enough to send by itself, halfway round the world. She'd send him a present. Christmas was only a few weeks away and by the time a parcel reached its destination it could merge with the seasonal mail. But what to get for a man twice her age, a man she'd never met – except on paper and then fragmentally, enigmatically – what to give her hero?

Men were always difficult to buy for. Even John, whom she thought she knew inside out, even he was a problem when it came to presents: novelty gifts got him worried about hidden meanings; personal luxuries were scorned as extravagance; practical items – tools, kits, gadgets – were met with more immediate appreciation but ended up cluttering kitchen cupboards; clothes were hopeless. Though he moaned enough about what he had to wear, her attempts to brighten up his wardrobe had always failed: some detail – buttons, cuffs, collar, lapels – which she had overlooked, relegated the garment to years in a drawer.

Through green silk jungle fronds, a black, gold-eyed panther snarled out from the rack of paisleys, florals and polka-dots, incisors gleaming, claws extended. The tie was almost as lurid as the cover of *Lair of the Panther Princess*. Luis Fortuna would love it. Or at least get a laugh. It weighed next to nothing, was easy to package, unbreakable. And on sale.

It was all ready to go: the note slipped inside crinkly tissue, the parcel wrapped, brown-papered, an additional note to the publisher clipped to one corner, the encompassing Jiffy bag stamped, addressed, sealed, hidden. She didn't want a lecture from John on the futility of spending good money on a complete stranger. Out of sight, out of mind, and the daily battle to keep domestic muddle at bay resumed its stranglehold on her attention. News stories hit the headlines and slipped off the back page before she'd caught sight of them.

She unfolded the newspaper cutting John had tucked under the teapot. A weather forecast? Two boxes — AFTERNOON and NIGHT. Small maps of the UK, scattered with clouds, directional arrows indicating winds and the occasional sunshine sputnik. Lighting Up and High Tide Times, Motorway Information and Satellite Predictions. A typical Met. Office report. Nothing out of the ordinary — no felt-tip arrows or stick figures or messages. Normal conditions for the season. Snow clouds looming over the north, motorway fog warnings, a sunny patch around the south-east. What was she missing?

She turned the paper over and saw it, the thick plain typeface, the solid black word: OBITUARY.

. . . from complications resulting from a minor operation, Luis Fortuna, best known for the highly successful film of his novel . . . a small town boy from a Pampas town . . . a homosexual who never hid behind the skirts of an ideology . . . died a dollar millionaire . . . was going through a bad patch with José, his rough young lover . . .

He would write no more books. Her free time would never be the same again. There was nothing to be done and no use blaming herself for being lazy or indecisive or reticent, it wouldn't have made any difference to anything. And maybe she'd got him all wrong anyway. It had never even occurred to her that he might be, have been, gay.

*

# Jumping into Bed with Luis Fortuna

She held the proof in her hands. She was settled and he was dead. It hurt, finding out hurt; not loud, public pain but an emptiness, an absence. This was it. Perhaps half-way across the world someone would sit in a darkened room and grieve for him but there would be no spectacle on his behalf. He was not a president, a rock star, a magnate. Perhaps a biography would appear, an unfinished novel but otherwise it was finished.

\*

Christmas morning begins too early. The kids can't contain their excitement: it cracks and fizzles through the house. It's as well to postpone breakfast and get going on the presents: two big piles for Kate and Josie, two small bundles for mum and dad, a growing mound of discarded wrapping on the carpet. John picks up a small, neat package. Wearing an enthusiastic smile, a fatherly pretence, he tugs patiently at the knotted gold twine.

– That's just an extra. Leave it till later, she says, but he undoes the string, pulls back the tape and flicks the tissue into the air with a flourish. The tie which had been chosen for Luis Fortuna drops on to the carpet. Her husband picks it up. He drapes it over his wrist, holds it at arm's length, up against the neck of his shirt, looks at it for a long time.

– You don't like it, she says.
– I didn't say that.
– You didn't say anything.
– I like it. It's quite something.
– But it isn't you, is it?
– I didn't say that. I'm just . . . surprised.
– Open something else.

The kids pause briefly to glare at their parents: precious moments are slipping away in boring, grown-up talk.

– It's a beautiful tie and that's that, says Kate.

– Cat, says Josie.

– Panther, says Kate.

John wears his tie for Christmas. Throughout the day, as they act out their synchronised roles as parents, doing what they can to make the day pass peacefully – playing with the kids, taking a walk to the swing-park, cooking, eating and clearing up the dinner, slumping in front of Disney re-runs – she catches sight of John as he stops in front of mirrors to inspect his reflection. She too is surprised. She finds her husband strange, attractive.

# Human Interest

The noon sun shoots through the window of the Queen's Hotel
Bar and a thin rod of hot light bores into the dark mahogany table.
Before Julie is able to set down her shopping bag – between the
empty beer glasses and full, filthy ashtrays – Sam Cox has his
broad, stubby hands in it and is pulling out a wad of chapatis, a
pineapple, two tiny cooked chickens, a tub of buffalo curd.

– Hasn't she done well! says Alphonse. He curls his arms round
Julie's waist and eases her on to his knee where, after bending
forward to smack Sam Cox's hand away from the supplies, she
settles briefly.

– Good on you, kid, says Findlay Sneddon. I'd say a wee toast is
in order, eh Alfie? One for the road?

Alphonse raises his eyes to the ceiling, points at the bar clock.
Joan fires a column of cigarette smoke across the table.

– What *did* you do to lay your hands on chicken? Or are we not
allowed to ask? says Joan.
Julie giggles, springs to her feet, picks up the picnic and leads the
way out of the bar.

The sky is a vast, white glare. A map is spread across the

dashboard of the jeep. With one hand Julie holds down the flapping sheet. With the index finger of the other, she follows the twists and bends of a road, the only road, going north. Alphonse drives. His shirt sleeves are rolled up to the elbows, his dark glasses spattered with the corpses of small insects. In the back, Findlay Sneddon sleeps off his lunchtime beer, Joan and Sam Cox smoke and pass a water bottle between them.

Apart from the occasional rickety buffalo cart or sleek dark limousine, the road is empty. Due to recent events, normal travel on this road has been severely curtailed. Only those with urgent need to reach family or friends cram into the sagging, bulging buses, resign themselves to being driven at full throttle, to duck and pray at the sight of any approaching vehicle, to be hurtled round blind bends, a sheer drop on one side of the road, the threat of ambush on the other.

*This is stark, open country, contrasting sharply with the sun-drenched beaches and lush tropical vegetation of the south, which formerly lured tourists from colder climes. Tourism, in fact, had only recently increased to the point where it accounted for 40% (check) of the gross national product (is tourism a product? subst. income?). The rhododendrons and Scotch pines – planted by homesick Brits (in the early days of the Raj?) – are thinning out, the sugar pink and powder blue ranch-style bungalows giving way to flimsy shacks huddled along the roadside. There is little sign of life from these sad little thatched hovels. It is as if the invisible occupants are holding their breath . . .*

Joan taps the back of the driver's seat with her pen.

 – Alphonse, sweetie, says Joan, How about stopping for a quick look? Stretch our legs. Piccy or two. Calm before the storm and all that.

– Or the aftermath, says Alphonse.

Findlay Sneddon opens his eyes as the jeep skids to a halt.

– Background, says Alphonse. Want some?

– Thanks, says Sneddon, But no thanks. A bite to eat wouldn't go wrong.

– That lot's got to last until tomorrow at the earliest, says Julie.

– Besides, says Joan, Today's the lady's birthday, after all, and who wants crusts and chicken-bones for their birthday tea?

Julie gets down from the jeep, smoothes out the creases in her shorts, fondles the focus ring of her camera. Good legs, Sneddon observes. Neat little arse too. If somebody else hadn't got in there first. Young and new and oh-so-keen, just about wetting herself every time she catches a whiff of copy. Unlike some. As the others scout around, he extracts a chapati from the packet, tears off a piece, inserts it in his mouth and chews, with contempt.

Crouched down, going in for close-ups, knees parted, smooth honey-gold thighs against rough dry dirt and criss-crossed cane wall, a bowl of chillies left to dry in the sun, as fierce a shade of red as her lipstick. A satisfying composition of colour and texture. A fetching little scene. Fuckable, thinks Sneddon, definitely fuckable. But then he always finds himself thinking about sex *en route* to an assignment.

The shacks appear to be deserted. Doors swing open at a touch. The dark interiors give out a rancid odour. At the entrance to one lies the infested carcass of a dog. Julie clicks away at bits and pieces until Alphonse, resting a hand on her shoulder, advises her to go easy on the still-life compositions. There's a chance of a big story up ahead, a big, fast story where every split second might offer up a new angle and the last thing she'd want is to be taking time out to reload. Action is what they're here for. It's what they live on, how they eat.

*The sun is merciless. The paddies and plantations are behind us. There is neither a scrap of shade nor a breath of wind. Ahead the vista is dry rolling scrub, cracked earth and bleached outcrops of rock, like some elemental graveyard. And, indeed, in this endless desert, nothing seems to be alive except us and we're not in the best of shape. Throats parched, nostrils clogged with dust, heads throbbing from the pulsating glare, clothes crushed and sweat-sodden, exposed areas of skin sticking to hot upholstery, bellies rumbling. We fantasise about food and the supplies in the back – procured with considerable difficulty by our enterprising photographer – present an almost unbearable temptation. On my left, the truculent Scotsman constantly mops his face with a hanky. On my right, my old buddy from Boston hogs the water bottle. In the front, the photographer and the driver are too listless to pursue their ongoing romance . . .*

— You can't say that, Joan.

— Hmmmm?

— That last bit. About our lovebirds.

— My readers will eat it up. It's what they want. Human interest. A bit of life ongoing. In the midst of crisis, what is more uplifting than a budding romance?

— Even you must be able to see that it's out of context.

— Listen, Sam-Sam, too many hard facts and my readers turn over to Food, Fashion and Fiction. Still, out of respect for your unwavering sense of propriety, I'll give it a query.

The sun is going down and the sky takes on the quality of a sluggish, churning liquid, as the dust does its hazy aerial dance. Visibility is poor. Without switching on the headlights, Alphonse

continues in low gear along the deeply furrowed dirt track. He stops
the jeep behind a mound of rubbish and switches off the engine.

– Charming spot for a pit stop, says Sneddon.

– This is it, you cretin. Our destination.

A short distance away is the village; no more than a dozen
shacks, clasped in a bracelet of tiny fields.

– Helluva quiet, says Sam Cox.

– Looks like it's all over, says Sneddon. He leans forward and
prods Julie between the shoulders. In which case, dearie, I'd
suggest you get a big swig of the local gutrot down you before you
leap in with your glass eye.

– I've seen dead bodies before, says Julie, adjusting her lens to
the fading light.

– Yes dear, says Joan, But there are dead bodies and dead
bodies.

– Aye, says Sneddon. Whole ones and ones with bits missing.
Broken jigsaws of bodies. Bits you couldn't put a name to.

– Just cut it out, mate, says Alphonse.

– Only telling the truth, *pal*.

– Try putting it in print. Try that for a fucking change.

– Boys, boys. No fighting, please, says Joan.

The light has almost drained from the sky when the reporters
reach the edge of the village. Apart from the thin bleat – of a child
or animal it's not certain – and the rasping crackle of their own
footsteps, there is barely a sound.

– Evacuation? says Sam Cox in an undertone. Joan indicates a
thin coil of smoke.

– Another bloody red herring, I'd say, says Sneddon. Might as
well get it over with and get down to the food, eh? I could eat an
elephant.

# Red Tides

No one answers the lumbering man in khaki fatigues whose pen swings on a chain from his thick, red neck. There's a general feeling of indecision. No one suggests splitting up. If there had been something happening, if there had been noise, action – they'd expected troops, stone-throwing kids, mothers with babes in arms running down the street – they'd have been up and away on their own, propelled by adrenalin, fear and the promise of money. But there are no streets here, only narrow tracks between black, empty fields. It is too quiet.

At the flickering heart of the village burns a small fire, the only apparent source of light or heat. Around it, the villagers are gathered, sitting or lying on the ground. Here and there a limp figure is briefly lit up by the flames it stretches towards, before becoming once more absorbed into the still, silent congregation. There is a hazy, unreal quality to the scene; the twitching flames, the smoky air, the hush. What the reporters are witnessing is not another eruption of the trouble which has been flaring up elsewhere, not the terror of night raids, but the life of an entire community reduced to terminal torpor. Slow motion is what has happened to this isolated village on the dry plains.

*Above the fire hangs a cooking pot filled with boiling, stinking roots. Those who have the strength to crawl, scratch at the hard ground in search of insects. There is nothing else. The village has run out of food. The crops were torched by soldiers or rebels, no one seemed certain. They came at night, lit up the sky with fire and left. In the morning the fields were black as night. Bloodshed has passed by, but not the protracted agony of starvation.*

\*

# Human Interest

Several miles from the village Alphonse pulls the jeep off the road. Findlay Sneddon unpacks the food from Julie's bag and begins to pass it around. Joan takes a small candle from her purse, pushes it into the centre of a chapati, flicks a flame to the wick, holds up the token cake:

> *Happy birthday to you,*
> *squashed tomatoes and stew*
> *Bread and butter in the gutter,*
> *happy birthday to you.*

Julie snuffs out the candle with her fingers, pushes away the food held out to her, bites her lip until she tastes blood.

– If I eat anything, she says, I'll throw up.

– I wouldn't count on it, says Sneddon. He bites into a chicken leg. Your guts might be more pragmatic than your conscience.

– Fuck you! Julie's voice is thin, brittle as glass. Fuck the lot of you. Knew fine what they wanted. Staring you in the face, in every face. Doesn't need translation. Same in any language . . .

– A dreadful business, says Joan.

– The eyes, flies gorging on babies's eyes, heads drooping like dried-up pods. You sit here stuffing chicken into your faces while back there they're filling their mouths with mud. Are you going to put that in your columns? Are you going to tell your readers that?

– We really couldn't help, says Alphonse. Sometimes you just can't. Not directly.

– Might have made matters worse, says Sneddon. Got them killing each other over a few chapatis. Or us. Think about it.

– Did nobody ever teach you, says Alphonse, Not to speak with your mouth full?

# Red Tides

Sam Cox looks into the darkness. Something out there is moving. Lean, dark bodies circle the jeep, picking up their scent, the smell of food.

# Sapphires

It's early on a Sunday morning. Nobody in the world ever phones Joyce at this time except her mother, assuming rightly that she or Malcolm will be up for the children and wrongly that it's a good time to talk.

– Well, Hi. Roper here, Jack Roper? Ever spare a thought for little old me now you're safely back in the old country again? Just thought I'd give you people a buzz but now I'm talking I'm thinking, I don't know what time you got over there on that poncy little island of yours. Sorry – don't take it personally, sweetheart.

Sitting down, she wraps her dressing gown round her knees and curls her toes round the bar of the chair. She hasn't got her slippers on and the hall floor is cold. The TV is beaming Bugs Bunny into the living-room, appealing to one child but not the other and providing a good enough pretext for a squabble.

– Guess it must be morning with you people, breakfast time?

# Red Tides

It's the small hours here, I can tell by the silence. What I came for, but these days silence bugs hell out of me. Gimme noise, any damn noise. A chainsaw's as good as windchimes, boat roaring across the straits better than birdsong. Dead of night's a killer.

Sunday morning and she's listening to Roper, of all people, at the end of his Saturday night.

— Kids okay? And the man? Miss the bastard, that's the God's honest. Sleeping off last night's booze, eh? Lucky sod. A mate, he was, good drinking buddy, never one to call a halt to the proceedings. Not easy to find out here in the health-crazed Pacific sticks, somebody who can stay the pace. Man after me own heart.

— That part of me, that vital organ is still pumping away good style while the rest of the old corpus is packing up all over the shop. Still got me marbles. In two minds about the advantages of being clear-headed at a time like this, mind you. A bit of senility might come in handy when it comes to preparing to meet thy maker.

— Who's on the phone?
— Can I speak?
— I'm speaking first, I asked first.
— No you didn't.
— Well I got here first.
— I want to speak.
— Who is it?
— Jack Roper, she gives in. He's phoning all the way from Canada. D'you remember Canada?

# Sapphires

The children look vague and Joyce remembers that the big one was very little at that time and the little one still in the womb.

– Say hello, then let your sister speak, she says, passing over the receiver. Maybe they'll cheer him up. Or cut short the conversation. The big one blethers for a bit before she remembers that Bugs Bunny doesn't live on the TV screen forever and runs off to catch the end of the cartoon. Still in awe of the telephone, the little one tries a halting hello. At Roper's gruff reply her lip quivers and she yanks the receiver away from her ear as if it had bitten her.

– Don't like the man! Don't like the man! she bawls, clambering on to Joyce's knee and driving her skull into her mother's chest.

– What did I do? says Roper.

– She's just got a thing about men. Don't take it personally.

– You should see about that.

– She'll grow out of it.

– Some people never do, says Roper. But sanity, sanity! The friggin word makes me think of hospitals. Sanity, sanitary, sanitised. A sane, sanitised mind. One with clean, disinfected surfaces. For the foul bodies to feast on. Given the choice I'd trade me marbles for me balls any day, know what I mean? Gimme a lethal dose of libido. Shit, has that area of me anatomy been a lost cause lately.

– Not that Julietta seems to mind. Prefers it that way, I guess. Weird, really, she's such a sucker for lost causes and all. Show my wife a campaign with No Hope daubed all over it and she'll embrace it. The local peace movement loves her. She makes the best placards, sings her very own No Nuke songs as the drill sergeant screeches at his cadets to get the Raging Grannies out of his face. Got herself jailed one time for knocking a soldier into the sea. For a peace protester, my wife is some fighter. If I had her on my side . . .

Joyce struggles to prevent the squirming child from disconnecting the phone. Her dressing gown unwraps itself. The cord slips off and snakes around her cold feet. She can think of better things to do than shiver in the hall talking to a Saturday night drunk on a Sunday morning.

 – They've got a point, these peace people, I'll say. But all those meetings on top of a full-time job, my wife is never home. But what's with you people? Still find time for the conjugal rights? Still fit in the odd frolic since the family extension? Another girl, eh? Woman of woman born. Fed her yourself, did you? Gave her an intravenous aversion to the male members of the species? Reserved your tits solely for the use of another newborn girl-child.

Joyce stifles a groan. If Roper weren't dying . . . She considers the wisdom of waking Malcolm. After all, he'd been Malcolm's drinking buddy, not hers, not really. Not when she could help it.

 – Poor old Malc, eh? Ancient history but I still remember it: when Julietta was breastfeeding, she wouldn't let me near her. Come to think of it, she's never really been keen since. Shit. And our kids are grown.

There hadn't been a lot of choice in whom they'd met and Roper, in his blustering way, had sought them out. She couldn't just cut him off. The man was calling long-distance – dollar a minute –

and was, after all, dying. Dying when they'd first met him and still dying.

 

– Don't mind me talking, do you?

– No, no . . . she says. I'd get Malcolm except . . . it's really quite early here and we take turns for a lie-in on Sunday . . .

– Hell, no. Leave the lucky bastard to his kip. I just sunk a few beers and don't feel sleepy. Against doc's orders, of course. Nobody's gonna call me a party-pooper – though I did quit a bit before last call. The limit has to be drawn somewhere and if you don't do it yourself, some bastard insists on doing it for you. Trouble is, my limit's scraping the friggin ground these days.

 

Into one ear, Roper coughs and curses his lungs. Into the other, the wee one resumes her wailing aversion to the man.

 

– Too much of anything I like, I'm whacked as a dead fish. Nothing remotely strenuous on the agenda – no squash, softball, fishing. No sex either but what's new? These kickass medics want to turn me into a golf-and-bowls man and shit, it's not my style. What's a guy to do? Quit living to stay alive? Even my imagination has become a limp imitation of its former self.

– Jesus, it must be late here, very late and not that I really think Julietta is off out there screwing some lusty young tree-lover – but who knows. I ask myself, Would it matter now? Would it ever have mattered? Shit, who gives a damn. All I know is it's very late, she's not home, my lovely wife – no, not lovely. Julietta tells me *lovely* is a demeaning little word. Shit-hot on the nuances of language, my wife. Not lovely, beautiful. My wife is beautiful. Always has been, always will be. Julietta will be beautiful when she's eighty. By which time I'll be a friggin faded snapshot.

Joyce remembers Roper's wife with more affection than him, though they'd met only a couple of times.

– Send Julietta my love, she says.

– Sure, says Roper. When I see her. My wife has her own life. So she should. Gonna need it. Don't mean to be morbid, sweetheart, but I just got home from the hospital – via the bar. After what those bastards put me through, I needed something. Shit, you go in with your fists up, all set to fight the sick cells and hold out against the pain. But no way are they doing any of that stuff to me again. Not even guaranteed to work. Long shot, they say. Friggin dog's chance in hell is what they mean.

It's the job more than anything that's doing me in, but the docs won't write me off. Tell me I need the friggin routine I hate to keep me on my feet. The college won't grant a pension until I'm on my hands and knees. How's that for charity? Drag a dying man back on to his feet, make him slog out his last precious days to clinch the friggin insurance deal. A year, they told me tonight, at the outside. Imagine it. Imagine yourselves a year from now.

– I can't, says Joyce.

– Maybe, like my wife, you'll have taken up campaigning to keep young Malc off your ass. Shit, sometimes I wonder why God gave us guys pricks. There must be an easier way to perpetuate the species. I'm not knocking my wife – Jesus, some joke, eh? – great girl, good wife, and mother – the boys love their momma – but people change. Don't really remember who changed first. Too long ago.

\*

Julietta; a lively, dark-eyed woman who showed little sign of buckling under Roper's illness, or his ego. Maybe she called him *love* a little too often. She touched him a lot, in company, wore vibrant colours and shiny earrings.

– A year, *if* I keep my nose clean. Well, I say, screw the job and see the world. This place is fine for raising kids, building a home and getting on with life. But the kids raised, house built, what is there to get on with? Maybe I'll drop in on you and Malc for a couple of days. On my way to Paris or Rome. How about it?

– Of course, Joyce replied, I'm sure Malcolm would be pleased . . . though it's not very relaxing around here.

She wasn't at all sure, but what could she say? She let the little one roar down the phone to underline her point.

– You wouldn't recognise me now, sweetheart. Used to enjoy a good nosh but now it's pills with everything. After a lifetime of cultivating a paunch, I can see me feet again. And all the bits in between. God's honest I'm skinny as when I was sixteen. Nowhere near as horny, though.

– Maybe just as well, says Joyce, laughing.

– Laugh again. Go on. Sounds good. Warm. So near. Isn't the telephone weird? Don't you think it's creepy hearing a voice in your ear and knowing it's coming from half-way across the world? Wish you were here, as they say.

– How much have you had to drink, Roper?

– Too much or too little. Don't take it personally, sweetheart, I'm just sitting here looking out on black water and sky. On me tod. Didn't get along too badly, you and me, did we? When your hubby and my wife were tied up with other things, remember? All very amicable and above board. Except that night you were on strong beer and got plastered and weepy. Remember?

    – Vaguely, says Joyce.

She makes no effort to focus the memory but it sharpens up anyway. A stupid evening, consumed by drink and maudlin inanities. Should she remind Roper that he'd promised her sapphires that night? Sapphires, Christ. To match her bleary blue eyes. It had been that kind of night, wrong from the moment Malcolm left to give his class and Julietta rounded up the Raging Grannies for a dawn raid on the US navy base. Roper had been in need of company. She knew he was ill, very ill, in pain but he'd played on her sympathy and her drunkenness, pawing her body and slavering rubbish into her ear. After that night, she made sure she was never alone with him again.

    – Are you dressed yet?
    – What?
    – It's morning over there, right? Are you dressed?
    – Not yet. But I'm not undressed, if that's what you mean. Fully covered up, says Joyce, tightening the cord on her dressing gown. And a jealous toddler in my lap.
    – So what do you have on?
    – Christ, Roper, mind your own bloody business.
    – Go on, get angry. I like it.
    – Fuck you, Roper.
    – If only you would. Know what, sweetheart?
    –

    – Me prick's leaping up like a dog on a leash.

# Sapphires

Over an enjoyably late breakfast, Malcolm hears an edited version of Roper's call and can't quite work out why Joyce is so down on the dying man.

# Tracks

It was a driver's town, a town of rusty Chevvies and gleaming red Toyota pick-ups, sleek black Buicks and dune-buggies – though there were no dunes – with their innards exposed, smoking up the highway like motorised lobsters. The beat-up and souped-up, Rent-a-Wreck and Customised Comfort. Hub City, the residents called it and shook their heads in sympathy and disbelief when she told them she didn't have a driver's licence.

Sometimes she took the bus but it got to her, it really got to her: taking the bus made it feel like everybody in town was old, sick or deranged. Or too young to drive. Taking the bus made her feel there was something wrong with her too. The route took in the hospital, the Silver Birch Sunset Home, the HoneyBee Community Hostel and the Reservation.

There was always an oddball or two. Not that the bus was rowdy – a couple of weirdos goofing off didn't amount to a serious problem but you couldn't tune out, couldn't just be going somewhere, you had to be involved in what was happening inside, even if your part was just watching, being a pair of eyes taking it in. Somebody was always looking for attention, doing their number. Not that she'd ever seen anything really off the wall, nothing totally loco, not the kind of stuff they put you away for, these people hadn't lost the place altogether, just tuned into some crazy wavelength and got stuck there.

Somebody was always talking out loud, to everybody or nobody, or doing stuff to themselves most people did in private. Or just draping themselves over a seat in a stupid way, a way you couldn't ignore, had to look at and then away because once you'd seen the sideshow what else was there? So you looked out the window at the view.

It was a good view: the water flat and calm, far-away mountains, snow caps pink and gold at sundown. Like a picture postcard. But on the bus you didn't take it in. There was always some distraction, you couldn't get away from noticing the details, the oddball details, there was something about the bus, the lighting maybe, especially as it was getting dark, when the fluorescent tubes highlighted every scar and scab, whisker and bristle, tic, twitch, crease and stain. Taking the bus got to her so usually she walked.

There were three possible routes: the scenic route, the highway and the short cut. She had been in town long enough to give the scenic route a miss. It was getting colder out, darker, lonelier. You didn't take the waterfront walkway if you had to go someplace downtown. You went there for exercise, lungfuls of salty air, a look at the water. She'd gone there herself just to walk. New in town and nowhere to go, she'd spent hours each day walking round a town designed for drivers.

She hated the highway, the choking, toxic fumes from six lanes of traffic, hated being blown sideways as the logging trucks thundered past the Castaway Hotel, the 7-11, gas station one, gas station two, Walter's Waterbeds, Nick's Pizzas, The White Spot, The Rest Ezy Funeral Home, the liquor store. The noise and dirt on the highway got to her, cyclists cut in without warning, the sidewalk narrowed to nothing at the bridge, it was a bad place to walk altogether, it made you tired and hassled and wish you had taken the goddamn bus after all. And still quite a long way round, compared to the short cut.

The short cut was along the railroad which ran parallel to the highway, set back a good distance. It was high and quiet and near as she could get to the right direction. It got her to Maria's in half an hour. There was an open stretch at the beginning but most of the way the single track's coarse gravel banking was overgrown with blackberries. The town was full of them. And crows. A town of blackberries and crows. On the waterfront the berries were fat, juicy, sweet but up on the railroad they were tight black blisters, covered with a greasy dust from the trains.

For a hundred yards or so the banking shrank in against the rails. On either side of the tracks the ground fell away sharply. It was a long dizzy drop to the coiling river with nothing to grab a hold of but thorns. In summer, when the bushes were thick with leaves and blossom, they might have been like scratchy cushions if the worst happened and you had to throw yourself into them to avoid a train. At this time of year, the twisted branches bare and brittle, it would be like throwing yourself into barbed wire.

She had been caught on the hop a couple of times, only just beating the train to the clearing at the level crossing. It had given them a laugh, the men from the roads department, who for months had been sloshing truckloads of red, peaty mud around the junction which coincided with the crossing. It had given them a laugh because she'd only just made it. And because it was like a cartoon:

# Red Tides

*

*Rubbernecked, bigfooted Olive Oyl loping across the tracks like an ostrich towards a tattooed roadman in a yellow hardhat. Swept off her feet as the train rounds the bend, and clangs past. Swept off her feet in the nick of time; tears of terror, tears the size of ping-pong balls bouncing out of her eyes, tears turning into lovehearts pulsing across the screen as the damsel in distress realises that the danger is over. Olive and her hero secured in a shrinking bubble as the credits roll.*

It was something to talk about at Maria's while she swopped her coat for an apron and splashed a couple of mouthfuls of coffee into a staff mug. A cosy, cluttered place, Maria's was perched above the highway, painted turquoise and pink, to look like a Mexican cantina. Inside, the walls were draped with embroidered rugs and sombreros. The tables were pushed close together so diners could talk across the aisles. The waitresses had to be skinny.

Being so far north, Mexican passed as exotic, so Maria's did good enough business, even if the menu was limited to variations on a theme – ground beef, chillies, sour cream, onions. It would have been fine without the onions but there they were, every night, bulging through the orange string bag, skins dry, papery, deceptive. The milky juice made her cry every time she chopped them, hot stinging tears which left her red-eyed.

Not that anyone except Maria and the waitresses ever saw her. She didn't leave the kitchen until her shift was over. Waiting tables, she could have made double or treble but it was safer being out of sight. Under-age. Illegal. In a small town close to the border. Sometimes there were immigration checks. Not that she was an immigrant, just a runaway kid who should still be in school.

# Tracks

She should have run further straight off. The town was too close to the island. The first goddamn stop, chrissakes. Friends of her mother's had been eating at Maria's the other night. She'd only meant to stop a couple of days until she got herself sorted out, thought about what to do next, do with the rest of her life. But then she'd met Wayne and hadn't thought of anything much for a while, except making the rent.

Nobody else is on the railroad. Usually there was somebody walking the high line, taking the short cut across this driver's town. If somebody else was on the tracks you reckoned a train wasn't due. Not exactly company but it made you feel less alone. Not safe exactly but strangers didn't bother her up on the tracks. People who walked the railroad were different from the waterfront walkers. They were going someplace, had someplace to get to. Even if it was only downtown or home from downtown, at least they weren't just roaming. It made her feel bad to see people roaming.

She'd been sheltering from the rain, in the mall, picking at a muffin, sucking on a milkshake and wondering how long the hundred bucks would last her. Been doing sums in her head when Wayne had stopped, grinned and bummed a cigarette. They'd got talking. She hadn't spoken to anyone in days and Wayne had been in no rush to go anyplace. She'd told him what there was to tell, except her age. Lied about that. Said she was eighteen. Come and stay at my place, he'd said, later. I could use some help with the rent.

The hundred didn't last long and whatever Wayne had he got through real fast. But she didn't mind Maria's. The waitresses were soft-spoken, flat-shoed women. Their fun was a pot-luck dinner, a couple of guitars and a bag of homegrown. Old hippies with teenage kids, they weren't pushy, didn't ask questions, except motherly stuff like, Did you eat? Could you use a ride home? Her own mother was like another species from Kathy and Diane, with their scrubbed faces, baggy skirts and long, unstyled hair streaked with grey. Somethimes she'd take a ride home with one of them, if Wayne wasn't picking her up – which he only did on payday – if Wayne was staying home or out with his buddies, getting wasted.

Wayne liked to get wasted, out or in. Sometimes it was better if he was out when she got home from work. At least she got some peace for a while to watch a talk show. Wayne hated talk shows. The ball-game and horror movies were all he'd bother with but she liked to hear people speaking, about anything really, she didn't mind, it was good just to hear a conversation.

The river is a broad white snake way down below her, like the belt her mother wore round her small waist, buckled a notch too tight. On the far bank of the river, a tumbledown jetty and a rotting shack sag into the water. The river is slowly eating them away. And if it wasn't water, it was forest ate things up around here. JAWS! Jimbo would yell at the trees in her mother's yard, raising his axe.

Nobody had ever talked at home, not like real conversation. Orders, yeah there were plenty orders: Gimme this, Take that away, Say something. Shut the fuck up. What was right one minute was wrong the next. Like living on a seesaw. Her mother's moods went up and down ten times a day. And then there were the boyfriends. Jimbo was the latest. Mr One Word. Wayne didn't say much either, not to her. Droned on to his buddies about baseball and hockey and rock albums, how many beers he'd sunk the night before and the drugs he could buy at the back door of The Globe.

If Wayne was out she'd watch a talk show – or listen anyway – and tidy up. She didn't like mess, though she'd lived in one as long as she could remember. She was sick of it, of waking up to full ashtrays, crushed cans, stacks of greasy pots, the rancid, suffocating smell of beer, smoke and old food, sick of tripping over her mother's high-heeled boots and balled-up sweaters, of crusts and dog hair and God knows what crud squelching between her toes, sick of finding nothing for breakfast but stale crackers and flat soda.

Wayne was a slob but there was only one of him. And he didn't bring his buddies home too much because they cleaned him out of beer. In her mother's house on the island there were always house-guests, guys mostly, who stayed anything from a night to half a year. Sometimes a couple would stop over and give her a couple of bucks to babysit their kids, while they partied with her mother.

If her mother had been happy with it all, she wouldn't have left. If her mother had been happy she could have handled the mess. And the noise. That new guy, Jimbo, was a real noise junkie. From the city. Her mother had picked him up on the ferry and griped about him from then on. The guy kept the radio blaring twenty-four hours a day. Even asleep he needed the noise. The man with the axe. He got up around noon, dropped some acid and chopped logs in time to songs on the radio, like that was what you did on an island. The guy was seriously loco. And she'd stolen a hundred bucks from him.

If her mother had been happy with Jimbo – or with any of the others – just for one day. Or without them, though she'd no sooner kicked a guy out than she began to feel lonesome. Her mother was too tied up to come looking for her daughter. She'd left a note telling her mother to be happy, not to worry about her. Tonight she'd left a note for Wayne saying the same thing.

She pressed her jaw to feel if it was still swollen. Last night Wayne had hit her, not for the first time. Wanted to do some deal with her pay and she'd said no. For the first time. Her face still hurt but the swelling had gone down a bit and she'd put Coverstick over the bruising. Could she tell Kathy and Diane she had toothache? They were the trusting kind. They'd smile and sympathise. Maria would fuss a bit and give her tequila to rub on her gums. Wayne had taken what he found anyway and stayed out all night. Though she'd worked for every cent, when she slipped the bills she'd hidden from Wayne into her shoe, and set off for Maria's, it felt like stealing.

The sky is purple streaked with red. Through the tangled blackberry barbs she can see the cars and trucks streaming along the highway. And behind the highway, way out on the water, the dark fuzzy shores of the island she won't go back to. She begins to skip along the tracks, leaping from board to board, playing at not letting her feet touch the gravel. Loco Loco Locomotive, she chants, Loco Loco Locomotive and it feels like a kind of high, thinking about a train, a train roaring round the bend without warning and wiping her out.

# Tony's Dream, Claire's Insomnia

SRI LANKA: *The Hill Country near World's End*

She should never have taken the journey. She should have stayed on the flat, coastal roads, played safe. There was enough to deal with, without vertigo. It was a long, hot, dusty trail. The skinny road snaked up and up, a miracle of engineering, testament to progress, a twisted rope through remote villages where small, still people squatted by the roadside in front of meagre pyramids of oranges, pineapples, dates. The driver drove like a man late for his appointment with fate, charging into blind bends then jamming on the brakes. By the time the bus reached the summit, Claire had seen the crushed, rusting corpses of a hell of a lot of vehicles which had taken the bends too fast. She was sick with terror, unable not to look down, down at the vast pulsing landscape which lurched up and slapped itself against the window at each bend. Going down would be bad but not as bad as going up. There was something to be gained from losing height.

Claire had first noticed Tony with irritation rather than interest: the voice too loud, frame too large. Clumsy and arrogant with it, elbowing his way through a bus-load of crushed, self-effacing travellers, to the rear, where the tourists had set up camp amidst backpacks, bottles of water and bags of food. There was no room for him but he planted his feet firmly in the aisle, nudged and kneed until he'd established his patch of floor, then bummed an orange from the placid woman next to her, who had enough to supply the whole bus. From the breastpocket of his safari jacket he whipped out a Swiss army knife and sliced up the orange. Tearing fruit from skin, he chucked the peel, piece by piece, through the open window. His aim was good, sure.

The bus jolted. Tony's head landed face down in Claire's lap. His legs crashed across her neighbour. He twitched violently, gibbered. His teeth locked on Claire's thigh. Claire grabbed his hair and yanked until his mouth sagged open. The bus rollicked round another hairpin. Bend by bend, Tony's body subsided into a dead weight, pinning the two women to their seats. Claire's leg hurt where Tony had bitten her but his weight had a steadying effect, put the brakes on her pulse and the roller-coaster panorama. Eventually he came to.

– It was inside the orange. A spider, a huge spider in that orange. I almost ate it!

– But you didn't, said Claire's neighbour. So please try to stand up now. You are squeezing my fruit . . .

BANGKOK: *Cow San Road*

The smoggy leftover heat of the day was trapped under a band of low cloud like a headache. The sky was small, the streets big and busy. Mopeds buzzed by strip-lit all-night kitchens. Rats and drunken policemen patrolled the hot alleys. Claire saw the feet drooping into the gutter. The shoes were familiar: stout, British brogues; sturdy, well-made, expensive shoes which were totally inappropriate for the climate. She looked more closely. Of all the people to run into again. Tony lay face down, snoring loudly, on the street outside Hotel Heaven, where he had paid for 8'x 8' of wall-to-wall mirror, a wheezing air conditioner and a crawling shower cubicle. His arms were wrapped around his head. His room key was in one fist, the neck of a near-empty bottle of Mekong whisky in the other. Under one elbow was the remains of his take-away dinner. A colony of red ants had assembled and was methodically removing noodles, morsel by morsel, journeying across the alps of Tony's body *en route* to their food store.

– Boyfriend? said the muscular cop. He rubbed his gun obscenely.

– Not my type, said Claire.

– Bad boy. Go to jail, said the cop.

Had he done something stupid, lost the head and gone over the score with some girl or *ladyboy*? She'd seen other guys reeling back from the Patpong, gorged on sex shows, guttered on cheap drink, red eyes rolling around in their heads.

It was impossible to tell whether or not the cop was joking. He prodded Tony with the toe of his boot and continued to fondle his gun. Thai jails didn't have a great reputation – what jail has – and how would he cope, this phobic twit. If one spider could bring on a fit, what would being cooped up with a full-blown infestation do to him?

– He's a friend, said Claire.

– Boyfriend? Boyfriend?

– Tony. His name's Tony.

Without malice the cop slapped him and yelled in his ear.

– Go home, Tony. Quick quick. Or go to jail.

Between them, Claire and the cop hoisted Tony to his feet, dragged him off the pavement and propped him against the buzzer of Hotel Heaven.

LONDON: *The Northern Line*

Claire held tightly to the pole, trying to inhale as little as possible of the sweaty, suffocating air, determined not to give up her space near the door. The compartment was so crowded that there seemed no possible space for another body yet Tony pushed in and wedged himself against her. The tube doors closed. The train jolted and moved off.

– It's destiny, said Tony, when they got off at the same stop.

– Bad luck, said Claire.

They came out of the station into an icy wind.

– God, I miss the sun, don't you? said Tony. Can I buy you a drink, to make up for lugging a drunk to Hotel Heaven?

On home ground he seemed no more brash than anyone else. He put the palms of his hands together and bowed his head. Forgive me, he said. Or punish me.

She'd seen the gesture before; sitting at a table under a palm-frond roof, watching rats twitching their terrible tails a couple of feet above her head, she'd eaten her stir-fry. And witnessed the ritual humiliation of a local labourer who'd got a woman tourist so stoned she was rubbing herself up against a tree-trunk. The proprietor of Big Buddha Beach Hotel – a series of huts and an open-air restaurant – suspended preening his cockerels to see to it that everybody on site saw the labourer on his knees, begging forgiveness, without protest taking a fist in the face, a single blow which knocked him into the dirt.

Claire followed Tony into the bar. Anything to get out of the cold. Anything not to go home and punish herself. It was the end of a bad week. Redundancies were in the air and being the last in, it was likely that she'd be the first out. Worrying wouldn't do any good but she'd worry anyway. She'd lie awake at night, regretting all her extravagances; buying a T-shirt which she didn't absolutely need, taking a taxi when she could have walked, buying pizza when she could have made one for half the price. And the trip to Asia: at the time it had seemed so necessary to go exploring, necessary enough to ditch security and super-annuation, to take a risk. Now, with debts to pay and no certainty of paying them, it seemed ridiculous and futile.

They began to meet, for sex. Fierce, probing sex which left them dazed, fragile, exposed. Afterwards, they'd go out, to high places: bridges, flyovers, towers, the city had plenty to offer. Tony would take control, holding Claire when her legs buckled, head reeled, spinning tales about the view she couldn't bring herself to witness. Claire, for her part, brought along neatly wrapped parcels; inside each was a clear plastic box. Inside each box, a spider. She steadied him as he shrank in horror from her gifts. But when Claire could look down without crumpling in panic, when Tony was able to bear a spider clambering over the back of his hand, they found nothing to do but screw. Without the outings, the unwelcome gifts, the balance was lost and there was no forgiveness.

# Red Tides

TONY'S DREAM

The sun is eating into his skin, blistering the back of his neck, his forearms, his knuckles knotted around the flimsy iron rail which rocks at the slightest pressure. His feet, in open sandals, are also burning. The latticed iron veranda juts out from the wall of the cliff-top tea house. Through its open floor, he sees the swaying shadowy tips of tall trees. Needles of light jab his eyes.

– You're being very brave, Tony.

It is Claire. He knows it is Claire, but the woman whose image drifts behind him in the tiny wedge of shade could be anyone. But when he looks down again, when he can't stop himself looking down, all the way down, everything is so perfectly, seductively clear. There's a shallow patch of sea, a dazed turquoise disc which throbs and shimmers with the tide. He can see the seaweed below, and the glint of fish, though it must be how high? How can he be looking down, *so far*, how can he be so high up?

The metal rail cuts into his fingers. He's gripping the rail hard, squeezing but it's dissolving in his hands and, as it dissolves, he's floating off the veranda, wafting down towards that throbbing disc of water. But as he looks down again, gravity resumes its pull and he's hurtling towards the rocks. He screams but no sound comes out.

CLAIRE'S INSOMNIA

The body round and transparent, like a bead, or blister, suspended on bent black legs. It's the movement which makes it

158

disgusting, sinister, fascinating, the legs so thin they're invisible until the twitch of one registers on the retina, one tentative outstretched leg, testing the lie of the land, in this case the wall above her bed. The deception of that leg, the trickery of its thinness.

After it has made its misleading investigations, then frozen long enough to delude, it takes off without warning in another direction altogether. In an ugly burst of activity it proceeds: always obtuse, deceptive. Better at least to see it, to know where it is, than to imagine it making its manoeuvres under the duvet. She hasn't been scared of spiders since she was little, not with that numbing fear which makes nothing possible until the source, the cause is removed.

Harmless, completely harmless. This climate doesn't appeal to the sturdy, venomous varieties, hosts only the spindly, theatrical ones, those which like damp dusty corners of unheated rooms. But she won't be putting off the light, not unless it takes itself off to a far corner of this unheated room. Even then, where will it go exploring in the dark? She must smell like meat. And what else to do with those terrible legs than . . . not crawl, nor scuttle – in spite of its crab-like sidestep – no, the spider's a prowler, all set to advance from its corner and prowl over her. She gets out of bed and goes over to the window. Her new flat is on the tenth floor of a riverside development. It is a clear, still night and the view is breathtaking.

# Wing

– What I want to know is, what is wind? the woman barked into the stale air of the bus station waiting-room. She waved her magazine about. The pages fanned out and fluttered sluggishly.

– I mean, everybody knows what rain is, for heaven's sake, and snow, clouds, hailstones, volcanoes for that matter, but wind? Personally, I don't have the foggiest and when I think about it, it seems quite remarkable that I've lived so long in utter ignorance of wind.

Wing looked up from the floor, where his eyes had been tracing the interlocking loops of a length of dirty string. Apart from the old woman and himself, the waiting-room was empty. He smiled briefly, shyly, leaned across the table between them and picked up a motor magazine, which someone had left behind. In response to his smile, the woman coughed noisily, pushed back flyaway strands of hair from her wide, spluttering mouth and craned her neck in the direction of the door.

Wing turned pages filled with cars, campers, spare parts and accessories. He was not a driver. Never would be, if he could help it. Cars were dirty, noisy machines with no soul. So were buses, but his pushbike was broken, the pushbike which, by day, got him to college and, by night, to his mother's cousin's sushi bar, where he put on a gold waistcoat, black pants and a smile six shifts a week, while most of his classmates were studying, drinking or driving the streets, looking for action. If he ever became rich, he'd buy a sailboat. If he became unimaginably wealthy, he'd buy a glider plane. If the winds of change blew him some unexpected fortune.

The woman took off her glasses and let them swing between a bony finger and thumb. She peered at the window where a maple battered its branches against the glass.

– There has been rather a lot of it about lately, wouldn't you say? Wind, I mean. Keeps me awake at night. Unsettling. Makes me think my apartment building's going to fall down, though between you and me, that might be a blessing in disguise. Not what it used to be, not at all. Tatty. And noise! I don't sleep well, as a rule. Age has something to do with it, I expect. Young people should sleep while they can, instead of staying up all night having wild parties.

– But what I say is, there's too much change in the air nowadays, too much upset. Nobody's happy. Nobody takes what they get these days, and makes do. It's trouble trouble everywhere. Blowing the whole place away might not be a bad thing. Blow it away and start again . . . I don't suppose you could tell me what wind is, could you?

Wing smiled again and shook his head. Whenever possible, he avoided speaking the language of Canada. He disliked the sound of it, flat and bland as the prairies, though the woman's voice had a trace of hills in it. Still, he wasn't exactly sure what wind was, though he knew its ways.

*

# Wing

Since he was small, Wing had made kites. He'd made his first when he was six, with the help of his father who was home for the weekend – a rare occurrence – and not too tired or busy with work or drinking. Spring, and above Friendship Hill the Nagasaki sky was dark with fighter kites, dipping and swooping all day long, smashing each other to pieces. But it wasn't the destruction of a kite which decided the winner: it was cutting the cord, setting it free which mattered and even though the loser usually fell to the ground, ripped to shreds, Wing had always thought of this as a kind of victory.

He'd begged his father to help him build a kite, not a fighter, not yet, just a simple flier. As first his father refused, as usual grumbling about things he had to do. Then he suggested buying one, out of laziness rather than respect for the traditional skill. They argued for most of the morning but eventually Wing won and, through hot hectic streets, happily clutched his father's hand, as they went looking for materials.

The workshop was hidden away at the end of a blind alley and looked like nothing at all from the outside. Inside, though, it was like a magic grotto: finished kites dangled from the ceiling in rows, their tassels twirling at the slightest turn of the air. It was like being underwater, looking up at shoals of paper fish swimming in the draught. On a floor spread with unfinished designs the kitemaker sat, dipping his brush into a big bottle of ink while his wife calmly wound silk thread around bamboo kite bones. A tiny tranquil old couple, doing what they'd always done, in harmony, with no thought of change. In front of them, Wing's father was unusually calm; mostly he was in too much of a hurry, impatient for change.

As the kitemaker wrapped up a package of paper, bamboo, twine and a small pot of glue, Wing asked about the designs, what they meant, where they came from, how many kites the man had made in his long life. Every question was answered and each answer led to another question.

– A boy like yours would have been a blessing to us, he said, and explained how he had no son of his own, how he and his wife would one day be too old, how if the business were to continue, they'd need to find a boy to train.

– When I first opened this place, he said, boys would come in all the time, asking to be taken on. We didn't need help then and, anyway, we couldn't afford it. Now nobody wants to make kites. They want new, they want change, want to work in a big factory, to make cars and computers.

Wing could feel his father's impatience begin to return. He was smiling and bowing, tugging his son's arm, no longer listening to the old man, thinking about the time, thinking that it was time to go and get on with making the kite, to get on with what he'd promised to do, not to take pleasure from it but so that it would be done, so that he would have done his fatherly duty.

They walked home through the Sunrise Gardens. His father agreed to stop for five minutes, to watch the fish. Five minutes. It was always five minutes with his father and though Wing couldn't yet tell the time, he knew there wasn't much in it. He climbed on to the wall round the pond and peered at the water. The surface was starred with lilies. Below, the fish moved, swift and slim, their whiskery mouths gulping the muddy water. Wing decided he wanted a fish on his kite, a flying fish on a background of swirls that could be sea or clouds.

It had felt so rare, so special, that day, his father cutting rods and fashioning a frame while Wing cut and pasted paper triangles, the two of them sitting close, silent and occupied. Since that first simple kite – which had taken a good deal more time than his

father had bargained for and, in the end, barely got off the ground
– Wing had made countless kites.

When he was old enough to go downtown on his own, he'd
returned often to the kitemaker's workshop and helped out,
learning what he could. His visits were welcomed by the old
couple, who were becoming frail and began to rely on the
assistance of his young eyes and steady hand. By the time his
mother had given up on his too busy, too absent father and, with
Wing, left Japan to join cousins in Canada, he'd learnt a lot about
the ways of the wind.

– You see, the trouble is, there are too many people. All the good
things about this place had to do with space, being able to spread out,
put a bit of distance between you and your neighbour. That's what
everybody was after, in my time. But too many people jumped on
the bandwagon and spoilt it all here and now we're packed like
sardines again. Bloody nuisance, that's what I say, not that anybody
cares what I say. And that's another thing. When I was young we
listened to the old. Now I'm old, nobody gives a damn what I think.
When I tell the caretaker of the complex that if he doesn't do
something about the loose windows there's going to be trouble, all I
get is dumb glares or empty promises.

Before sleep, Wing liked to look at comic books, the kind in
which heroes and villains battled for control of the world with
ancient magic and space-age weapons. The men wore bodysuits
and exotic armour. The women wore bikinis and thigh-high
boots. Monsters came in all shapes and sizes: the steely and
muscular, the shapeless hulks, the hideously mutant. The comics
gave him ideas for kite designs. As well as waiting tables, he made
a bit of money from his kites. Students bought them to hang in

their rooms. Relatives bought them for their kids. Sometimes kids were rough with the delicate things, and broke them. Their parents would complain about money wasted.

– Why don't you use tougher materials, they'd say. People use PVC these days. Paper stuff is history.

Lately Wing had been bothered at night, not by the gales which blew cabbage and bakchoy off the street stalls, tore holes in store awnings and upturned trash cans. It was in quiet moments during the night, when even Chinatown was asleep, that he heard another sound, a cold hollow roar. He imagined an illustration: a writhing, tormented beast being dragged into the glittering depths of an iceberg. He knew it must be a truck passing the narrow alley-mouth, displacing air, causing an updraught and an echo which bounced along the walls. He knew it must be that but still the sound chilled him.

The woman was staring at him.

– Very quiet today, don't you think? Normally you get all sorts hanging around here, loitering their lives away, pouring out their troubles, spilling their beer and blowing smoke into your face. Why they don't take a bit more care of themselves, I don't know. I'm no health fanatic but I do use the pool in the complex every morning. It makes sense, doesn't it? But some of them, you'd think they'd no homes to go to, which is probably the case, judging by the state of them. Makes me wonder just how long this country can go on opening its doors to all and sundry. In my day, my day . . . but I expect I'll never know why a country chooses to set up something sensible and then mess it around. When I think about it, I've a mind to go back to England. But I'd miss the weather. Hah! What am I saying? It's wild out there. Can you see that tree, that red maple, the one they put on their bloody flag?

# Wing

Flailing about like a demented dervish, wouldn't you say? A wild wild wind. I expect that's something else I'll die in ignorance of.

*

The sun was out, the park busy. A faint but steady breeze stirred the leaves on the trees. Wing passed the animal houses and the popcorn stall, taking the path for the miniature garden. At the pagoda-shaped gate he stopped to read the eroded plaque:

TH S G RD N IS A G FT TO TH   CITY

FR M THE PEOP      OF JAPAN

WHO S TTL D H RE   N 191

Saltwater City, they'd called it when they first arrived by boat, as indentured labour, to work the shipyards, railroads, mills, mines, to cook for prospectors and wash their filthy linen.

Facing east, where a small statue of Lord Buddha smiled down on a mass of chrysanthemums, a slight, pig-tailed woman prayed. Lilies smothered the surface of the pond. The fish below were like those he remembered from the Sunrise Gardens – gold, silver and black with shiny round scales like coins – but bigger; fat, sleek, sluggish. Kids fed them popcorn. On the trellised wall a drab, dusty heron surveyed the pondwater without interest.

From the top of the hill, Wing could tast the salt in the air. A wave of white hotels swept round the sparkling city waterfront, tailing off at the bridge out of town. Under the bridge, on the far side, lay the logging and pyramids of foul yellow sulphur. Nobody liked to live downwind of the mine though plenty did. Like Chinatown, it was cheap. But the smell of sulphur got under your skin. He'd heard a girl at college say that before class, she'd sneak into a department-store perfumery and spray herself with the most expensive scent they had on trial. He hadn't got close enough yet to tell whether she smelled good or bad.

Container ships slid imperceptibly across the horizon: cars to Canada, wood to Japan. Wing unzipped his carrypack, spread the kite on the ground, ironing out the creases with a flat palm. One of his best, at least, his favourite. He listened to the wind sifting through the grass then stood up, turned, threw the kite into the air, jerking it back briskly, for lift. The cord unravelled through his fingers, stinging as the kite leapt and dived, tugging on the line like an angry black fish. He played it through a single loop then cut the cord.

# Red Tides

This day there's no swimming because of the red tides. At the town end, First Beach is covered with noxious algae the colours of rust and blood. A thick band of the stuff clings to the high-tide line like a scarf or a bandage. A big stretch of sand is messed up by clots and spatters. Sunbums have moved further along, making our patch less private than usual.

But it's a good day for the beach: hot, with a fresh breeze blowing off the water. Lois, Carla and I are face down, flat out on our towels. We're lying in a row, like a tanning chart – Before, During and After. I'm white and pink in bits, Lois is light honey, Carla is olivey bronze. We could soak up the sun all summer and our skin tones still wouldn't even up. We're different, that's all. Around us is the usual litter of clothes, tanning oil, snacks, cold drinks, cigarettes, books. We've been coming here between shifts since the good weather began. We've got our beach needs sorted out.

Carla and I do other things together when Jimmy's out of town. Lois stays home and waxes her furniture or her legs. Or dates Andrew who's definitely a hot number. The girl wriggles when she says his name, stretching the A around her mouth like gum. His name comes up a lot. Doesn't matter what we're gabbing about, Andrew has seen it, done it, or got an opinion on it. You can see the *frisson* rip through the girl every time she stretches that A. No problem in that, I mean, everybody likes a little jolt. But when you're between men the eternal mention of somebody else's really gets to grate and right now that's my story.

There's a piano-player in one of the wharfside cafes who's kinda cute – plays moody Van Morrison numbers and smiles to himself while he's tickling the ivories. Sometimes I drag Carla down there after the beer bars but I know she hates it. The décor's repro deco, straight lines everywhere, nothing fancier than the odd triangle, and that goes for the clientele as well. Basically, Dorothy's is full of jerks, but because it's pricey it's never so bombed you can't get a seat, and at the end of a shift that's something. I guess I'd have settled for the crush at the beer bars if it hadn't been for the little blond guy with the nimble fingers. Looks good in his tux. So who doesn't? Carla says. And you've only seen him late-night. This is true and I've been fooled before by candlelight, dimmer switches and booze.

The reason Carla and I don't go places with Lois – apart from the beach – is basically Andrew. She keeps the guy out of sight but can't shut up about him. We know his height: six/two; hair colour – chestnut (not just brown for God's sake, chestnut); eye colour – hazel – Andrew the nut, as Carla says. We know what kind of car he drives, what he likes to eat: littlenecks and bloody beef; how many times he brushes his teeth, what he likes about Lois – her body, hair, clothes, apartment, personality, in more or less that order. Lois tells all. Can't help herself. Andrew is way up on her priorities. Otherwise, she keeps her business under wraps. Like what she did before she moved to the coast. One time Carla asked her straight out. Lois closed her eyes, turned her neat nose to the side, blew a slim line of smoke through neat, glossy lips and said, Streetwalker – dead serious – Fall River.

We got the message. Sure there are places to be a streetwalker but Fall River is not one of them. Stinks of sulphur from the mills when they're open and hard times when they're shut down. This girl wouldn't drive through the streets of that town, never mind walk them. Her favourite slogan is a store sign outside a dry cleaners: GRIME DOESN'T PAY. And does she believe it. Her apartment has surfaces which glow like the heavenly bodies are supposed to and her soft furnishings have a nurtured look, like pets.

Lois has manicured blonde hair which turns into her neck in a single wave and looks metallic in the sun. She's pretty in a regular front-of-house way – even-featured, nothing lop-sided, nothing too big or too small, medium height, leggy, looks good in clingy T-shirts, skimpy sun-dresses and the high-cut frosted bikini she's wearing. She's undone the back strap and halter neck so she won't have any paler strips of skin around her tits. In case Andrew doesn't like it.

There are things we don't know about the girl. We do know she's recently divorced. Alan (another A name), the husband she ran after for years, ran off with a girl the spit of Lois but younger and with money. Lois threw all the frozen dinners she had prepared – a month's supply of planned, balanced meals – into the waste disposal and moved to the coast for fun, sun and fucking. What she got was Andrew.

After our shift at Neptune's, Carla and I sometimes go drink beer, listen to the band, bitch about this and that – the slow eaters, cheap tippers, the pains and the real assholes. Maybe we'll let some guys buy us a beer. But Carla won't fool around. It's not safe and she knows it, she's no fool. Jimmy drinks Old Bushmills and sings slushy Irish songs with some touring band, Retro- or Repro-something they call themselves and it's what they are, old-style fake. Jimmy's never been within a thousand miles of the Emerald Isle but turns on a brogue at the merest sniff of whiskey. And gets punch-drunk and jealous in a big way. Carla's a whole lot better than he deserves.

Our place in the sun is at the end of the comfort zone. Further along the coast it's too rocky for stretching out. There's a big cruising scene down by the changing huts but where we are, next to the big rock and high, scratchy dunes nobody can just stroll by and parade their tan and muscle tone. They have to say something and better have some good lines. Carla gets off on crucifying cruisers. She's right, sure. But sometimes when it's hot like this and there's nothing to do and the sand chafes the bikini line and grinds its way under the swimsuit legbands, mixing with slicks of tanning oil, sweat and other body fluids, I'm personally not in such a hurry to chase away an okay guy.

But here we three are on our own little tail of beach and who's there in the distance but Monsignor Zyw. The black skirts of his coat wing out as he picks his way over the wounded-looking beach. The Monsignor is a regular at Neptune's and everybody's favourite customer. What a treat he is, a real sweetie. And so easy – orders the same meal every time.

– The Scrod, bless your heart.

(Scrod – no such thing. It's a made-up name for baby cod, a restaurant fiction.)

But this little guy with his tinkly voice – who gets the giggles halfway through his second Martini – makes us all try to be a bit nicer than we really are. Even Gus. His usual cynicism crumples like a dishrag at the sight of old Zyw perched tidily at his table for one, hands clasped round each other, bird eyes sparkling.

– And how are you tonight, Father? says Gus.

He dips his voice to the carpet and tips a two-fingered salute at the worry waves rolling across his forehead.

– Wonderful, my son, Zyw answers every time, Bless your heart.

While Monsignor Zyw chews at his Scrod and the Ballams pick at their lemon-dressed salad and probe sensitive areas of their marriage, blind Bill likes to give us girls a hard time. We forget to turn our heads when we speak to him. Thinks we don't bother. Look at me, goddammit, he says. You think, what's he getting at? He can't see. But Bill can say exactly where your voice hits the wall. Tunes pianos. Looks like Roy Orbison.

– Take a look at who's cruising, says Carla to Lois, Doesn't it kill ya?

Lois takes forever to see the vertical, buttoned-up Monsignor among the horizontal bodies. When she does, instead of going coy and cutesy – like she does when she waits on him – her face goes kinda cloudy. I mean, I'm looking up thinking the weather's about to break but no, the sky is pure blue – then she's twisting about on her towel, hooking up the backstrap and halter, squeezing into a tight T-shirt (Lois doesn't own any baggy ones). Then she's stashing the book she's been reading, in her bag.

– Must be raunchy stuff, says Carla. Lend it to me when I'm feeling deprived.

– I could use it right now, I say.

Lois ignores us. She lies down on her back. A frothy red scarf lifts and ripples and veils her face.

We always bring books and read for a bit before we get too hot and sticky, before the print starts to jump in the sunlight and it becomes too much effort to turn a page. Carla picks racy new fiction and crime stories set in exotic locations. Lois goes in for sex disguised as romance or romance disguised as sex. Me, I never know what I'm looking for and never seem to find it. I get through a load of books. Don't read them. Start plenty but mostly give up quick. Short attention span. Or something.

– So what's the story? says Carla. Picking up tips on a new way to fuck, or what?

– I wish you wouldn't call it that, says Lois – who's no stranger to the word – It sounds so ugly.

– You want it to sound like eating ice-cream?

– I gotta go.

– No you don't.

– Ice-cream sounds good. Black walnut with blueberry ripple.

– Butterscotch fudge.

– Who's going to stand in line?

– Think you could give up sex if you had a constant supply of ice-cream?

– Think you could give up ice-cream if you had a constant supply of sex?

– Really girls, I gotta go.

– Things to do.

– People to see.

– Anyone in particular?

– No prizes for guessing.

– Please, says Lois, will you please knock it off?

Some nights just don't work out, however you look at it. It's like there's something in the air, some kind of virus which hits out at everybody. A hot day, a hotter sweaty night, the cooks stripped down to their vests, Gus running out of ice and running off at the mouth at blind Bill's sister. Somebody screwed up on the reservations. It happens. So what's the big deal? Everybody gets their goddamn dinner sooner or later but regulars don't like it, regulars get ratty real quick about folks from out of town taking their tables. The Ballams get stuck by the kitchen and jeez do they bitch and bicker and hassle us girls, sticking a fork in the air every time we go by. Monsignor Zyw gets wedged between the crabtank and the air-conditioner and the kitchen runs out of Scrod just before his order goes in. The night is lousy all round. By the time we get our aprons off we're ready to kill or sink some drinks and think about it. I'm speaking for me and Carla. Lois has other plans.

This town is too small. I mean first we meet the Monsignor on the beach – he finally gets through all those bodies to us, raises his hat, bows and walks around the rock, to peace and quiet and an empty stretch of shingle. Carla and I wave, Lois crosses herself. Chrissakes, we should have known something was up with the girl. I mean, it's just not something you do when you're wearing a bathing suit. After the dinner shift, our feet are burning up, I persuade Carla to start out at Dorothy's instead of ending up there and who do we meet but blind Bill. He's sitting right by the piano, alone at the best table, on the prawn-pink sofa. He picks up on our voices and calls us over.

Bill orders highballs for us without asking, pats the sofa on either side of him in invitation. Carla stays on her feet. I sit. The guy doesn't bother me. He's got some good stories about old jazzers he's tuned pianos for in New York City, I like his line about seeing with his ears, he doesn't say stupid things about what you're wearing or how you've fixed your hair. And I get to see the piano-player.

# Red Tides

Carla sucks down her drink.

– I'm out of here, she says.

Jimmy's doing a spot at O'Malleys. I've heard Jimmy's band enough to know I can miss it. And O'Malley's has the worst seating in town – high-backed pews some nut saved from a burning chapel and stuck in the bar when old-style was new. After tonight's shift, I'm happy to stick with the sofa.

Maybe Lois tried calling the bars, she knows where we go. Maybe she tried a couple and gave up. It's always the same, isn't it, I mean, where's anybody when you need them? More likely she couldn't get near a phone. On the beach, at work, she said nothing and Lois never liked to be asked. She'd tell you a thing in her own time, if at all. We should have known. But say she'd come looking for us, what would she have found?

. . .Jimmy going loco with a broken bottle, carving up Carla's ex for buying her a beer. Me out of it on the beach with Bill and the piano-player – Lyall – all three of us blind drunk, stumbling, lurching, swaying into another kind of craziness. Carla at the hospital, me on the beach, Lois out of her mind in her glossy apartment. Some night. Must have been a full moon or something, but I wasn't paying much attention at the time.

*

The sea is warmer than earlier in the summer, the beach clean and swimming good. These days, mostly, I'm alone, though once in a long while Carla joins me. Carla doesn't get out much and when she does, all she wants to do is sit in the dingiest corner of some tired, empty bar and worry about Jimmy. Something's got to give.

# Red Tides

Her ex now has a ragged scar across his neck and he's been spreading the word that Jimmy better quit town, which of course he won't do while he can still camp out at Carla's place, eating her food, drinking her booze etc. I reckon she'll go south at the end of the season, if she's still got it in her to make the break.

The red tides haven't been back and neither has Lois. She quit Neptune's and got herself some kind of day job. Andrew doesn't like her working nights and what Andrew doesn't like, goes. Her name comes up from time to time. Gus says she's giving out to half the cops in town. Andrew's father is chief of police. Andrew admires and fears his father. Andrew has a Dobermann, a shotgun and a taste for pain games. That day on the beach, the girl was reading de Sade. Nobody could say she wasn't prepared, but still. Lois. I reckon she's gone over the limit.

I miss the company down here, by the black rock. Just me and the gulls is getting kinda dull. I've given up books. Too much trouble. I eat, sleep and cool off in the water. The gulls clean up my crumbs before the breeze blows them away. We had some good times, the three of us, and when times were bad we kept each other from going under. Laying around, flaked out in the sun, it seemed like no matter what was happening in anybody's life – if we could just laze around and talk it through, or just talk, about anything, it didn't matter, almost any kinda mess could be straightened out. At the end of an afternoon, we'd take home our garbage, our oily, gritty towels, our hot tight skins. Also some kinda plan for the future: no big deal – some way to get by for a night, a week, month, season. A season at the outside.

I miss the girls. Don't miss blind Bill or the piano-player much.

## Red Tides

Don't remember much. There's a blank where there should be a weekend. Bill's eating someplace else these days and I steer clear of Dorothy's. Not much to miss, I reckon, either of them. Nothing I couldn't find elsewhere. But I don't know for sure and right now I've nobody to talk it over with. Maybe I should move further along the beach, meet some new people. Or on. Maybe move on.